The Strange Disappearance
of Mr. Toast

The Strange

Illustrated
by Leslie Goldstein

Disappearance
of Mr. Toast

by Stuart Brent

The Viking Press · New York

This book is for my children

The Strange Disappearance
of Mr. Toast

It seemed as though the most important day of the
year would never come.

The most important day of the year for the Brent
family was not a definite date that you could count on,
such as a holiday or a birthday. It was "sometime" after
school was out for the summer. For reasons the children were never able to discover, Father and Mother
always seemed to have great difficulty in making up
their minds just *which* day would be THE day—the day
the family would set out for Bark Point in northern
Wisconsin.

All through the fall and winter the whole family had Bark Point more or less on their minds. But with the first signs of spring they began to think about it all the time—all except Baby Joe, who was too little to remember.

Father would think about it every morning while driving to work in the city, down a big expressway, bumper to bumper with thousands of cars, and everyone hurrying to get to work on time. "By now the snow must be melting up north and the ice breaking up in Bark Bay," he would think. "It won't be long now."

Mother thought about it constantly—while she was getting the children ready for school and caring for the babies and planning the meals and making the shopping lists and doing all the invisible things that keep a large household happy. "The day can't come too soon," she would think, seeing someone's muddy footprints smeared across the kitchen floor.

David would look up from a book and stare across the high school study hall and out the window at the blue, blue sky, and think, "It can't be long now!"

Susan and John, erupting with a mass of children onto the school playground for recess, would notice that the ground was still frozen in the shaded spots and the air had winter's bite in it. "Bark Point day will never come," they would moan. Summer was still too far away to be imaginable.

When Amy studied the pictures of birds and animals on the kindergarten walls, she recognized many of her friends in the fields and woods around Bark Point. "Probably we'll be going tomorrow," she decided.

Lisa, the three-year-old, playing with Baby Joe on the living-room floor, felt the warmth of the sunlight striking through the window. It was just like a bright day on the shore at the Point, a day in the sun that goes on forever and ever.

The only member of the family who was not living in this fantasy was Mr. Toast. He couldn't be fooled by mere dreams or wishes. When summer was really here, Toast would know it. When Father and Mother actually began to plan the departure, Toast would be the first to get the signal. And when the family was at last on the road and the landmarks came into view showing that Bark Point was near, Toast would be the one to spy them all. Meantime, however, he had the heavy responsibilities that take up a dog's full time and attention.

All day long, Toast watched over Lisa and Baby Joe.

11

He let Lisa ride on his back, for he was a big and powerful dog, large even for a golden retriever. He allowed the baby to hug and kiss him, pull his ears, pat his face. But if any quarreling broke out between the two little ones, Toast put a stop to it with a few cuffs of a firm but gentle paw.

When the older children came home from school, Toast was always waiting to meet them. This was a joyful time of play and rough-and-tumble. Then when the hour approached for Father to get home from the city, Toast again prepared to be a one-dog welcoming committee. Whenever Father was late Toast became fretful, and when he finally arrived Toast was certain to be the first to greet him, dancing, wagging his tail, begging to carry the newspaper. Mother and the children recognized that this was Toast's privilege.

So every day was a very big day, even for as strong, as brave, as beautiful, as intelligent, as noble a dog as Mr. Toast. And every evening when the children were finally tucked in bed and Father and Mother sat quietly together in the living room, Toast would collapse by the fireplace, shut his eyes, sigh, and fall asleep.

David was the first really to begin to worry about whether they were going to the Point that year. School had been out for a week and not even a hint had been dropped about their summer plans. To be sure, the weather was cold for June—but not all *that* bad. Finally David had a talk with John to find out if he knew anything about the matter.

John's love and admiration for his older brother was intense, but as soon as he detected David's concern he automatically adopted an air of "don't care."

"Heard anyone say anything about going up to the

Point?" David asked. He tried to sound casual, but for David this was very difficult.

"I suppose we'll have to go—sooner or later," said John.

David could scarcely curb a burst of rage. He could already smell the clean northern air, the lake, the scents of field and forest. It was as though someone at the dinner table, namely John, had expressed indifference to a beautiful meal composed entirely of treats David had been dreaming of for months.

"Forget it," he said crossly. Then he noticed that John's smile was twisted and there was just the suspicion of tears in his brother's eyes. John's eyes always seemed to reveal what John was actually thinking.

"Forget it," David said again, but this time he patted his brother on the head and turned and walked off.

John went to look for Susan. When he found her and asked David's question she burst into sobs. "Nobody's told me," she said. "I think they're going to leave me behind!"

"Nobody would leave you behind," John said tenderly.

Susan knew this, but at the same time she had the feeling that something awful had gone wrong and that in some unknown way it might be her fault. Anyway, it was a great comfort to cry about it.

David, meanwhile, wandered out into the back yard and was glad to see Toast sunning himself and looking altogether at peace with the world. He sat down beside Toast. The sun felt warm, but the ground was winter-cold.

David put an arm around Toast and said nothing but just sat quietly thinking about Lake Superior—the great fresh-water ocean—where some of their neighbors at Bark Point, the old professional fishermen, took their small boats and their nets far, far out, like ancient seafarers. He thought of the woods and the hosts of small animals living in them—beavers, porcupines, skunks, foxes. He thought of the open country where there were deer, and of the scores of small lakes and brooks and rivers where the fishing was good. And most of all, as he sat in the sun with his dog, he thought of the great peace and quiet of the north country—the sun and the wind, the sky and the water, and the shade of the forest. Their cottage at the Point seemed to him to be their true home.

Toast thumped his tail and literally smiled. "He knows something," David thought. He was sure of it.

15

Toast already knew when they were going!

Toast had learned about it a few nights before. He was sleeping by the fireplace while Father and Mother sat reading. Occasionally they looked up at each other or glanced at Toast. Presently Father said, "Hope, shall we go for a walk?"

Mr. Toast opened one eye.

"Yes, let's," Mother replied.

Toast opened the other eye.

"Shall we go now?" Father said.

Toast sat up.

"By all means," said Mother.

Toast drew himself up, placed his paws on Father's chair, and grinned, squinting his eyes like a chow.

So together Mother and Father and Mr. Toast went out for a stroll. The Brent family live in a big, old house in a quiet suburb north of Chicago. All the houses stand among tall trees, and even when early June is cold the shaded streets are filled with smells of leaf and blossom. But almost *nobody* goes out for a walk, except the Brents and their dog.

"I don't see how we can possibly go up to Bark Point this month," Father said.

"Neither do I," said Mother wistfully.

"The children will be very disappointed," Father said.

They began to walk very slowly, and Toast walked slowly too.

"We may not be able to survive," Father said.

"I don't think we could," said Mother.

"Maybe the thing to do is just to go up anyway," Father said.

"I think we should," said Mother.

"Woof," said Mr. Toast.

"Then we'll leave next Friday," Father said firmly.

Mother smiled. "I've already begun to get the summer clothes in order. They'll be ready in time."

Mr. Toast bounded ahead in high glee. Soon he would be exploring in *his* woods, swimming in *his* lakes, exercising his *full* responsibilities as both family protector and master of field and stream.

"Mister Toast!" Mother and Father were calling him way down the block. Toast stopped so quickly that his hind legs nearly overran his forelegs. He pivoted around and raced toward them, ears tight against his head and his red fur flashing under the street lamps.

"Easy, Mister Toast," said Father, and they started

17

for home at a quiet pace but with their hearts quickening.

On the important morning, everyone was up before dawn.

The living room was piled high with suitcases and bundles and just plain stacks of "things." Every few minutes someone came in with a fresh armload to add to the collection. Mother was making breakfast in the kitchen while Father and David and John began carrying the luggage out to the station wagon.

Each time Father came in the door he would look around and shake his head hopelessly. No matter how much they carried out, there seemed to be just as many boxes and bags and piles of clothing stacked on the sofas or sitting on the floor.

Susan came into the living room, carrying a bird cage.

"Not yet," said Father, staggering out with a half-dozen satchels. Susan had the distinct impression that he was carrying one of them in his teeth, but this was probably because he was using his chin to help balance his load.

She went back into the dining room and put the cage

on the table. The familiar room seemed strange this morning, and when Mother called from the kitchen her voice had a kind of hollow ring. It was the way your voice sounds when you burst into the house shouting and there is no one at home. "I guess the house thinks we're gone already," Susan decided.

"Where's Lisa?" Mother wanted to know.

But Toast was already gently nudging the three-year-old out of the pantry.

"Now you keep your eye on Lisa and Baby Joe," Mother said. "This is no morning to have children disappearing." Toast made a rapid count of the small fry and went off to look for Amy.

"All aboard!" Father shouted at last.

It seemed impossible, but every bit of luggage was tucked away somewhere and there was still room for passengers.

In they all crowded. Amy sat in the front seat between Mother and Father. Joe knew it was really too early for a baby to be awake, so he curled up on Mother's lap and went to sleep instantly. Susan and Lisa shared the middle seat along with a good many packages, while David and John established themselves in the back. Toast gave the whole arrangement a careful appraisal and jumped in back with the boys.

"Everyone sit still now so I can check us out," David requested.

"Check yourself out. Let's go!" said John.

"We're off!" Father announced, and started the motor.

"Where's the bird?" David called from his vantage point in the rear.

"On the dining-room table!" cried Susan.

Father groaned. Then he tossed the keys to David, who went running into the house to rescue the canary.

"We're off," said Mother hopefully, when David, looking rather smug, had returned with the bird cage.

"I doubt it," said Father, but he started the car anyway, and a cheer went up from the occupants as they rolled out of the driveway and turned down the street.

"Shhh! The neighbors are sleeping," Mother said. "But hurrah, anyway!" she added, smiling.

They were soon out in the countryside. All their doubts about when they would go and their worries about getting started were over. By nightfall they would be in their cottage, taking up the life they loved best.

20

The sun was just coming up, shining through the little puffs of white mist over the fields. "It looks as though the world's just begun," Susan said.

Lisa gave a cry of glee. "Cows!" she said.

"Those are horses," Amy told her.

"Cows, cows!" Lisa insisted.

"She thinks everything's a cow," Amy said hopelessly.

"Give her time," said Mother.

"Cows," said Amy, to make sure the matter was settled.

"Tomorrow we'll go to Herbster for supplies," Father said, "and the next day we'll start planting the garden."

"It's late for planting," David said. "Everyone else's garden is in already."

"We'll catch up," Father said. "The days are long up north and the cool air is good for growing things."

"I can stay up late," Susan informed them. "It doesn't get dark until ten o'clock."

"If we lived there in the winter, you'd go to bed as soon as you got home from school," David told her.

"When it snowed, I wouldn't even have to go to school," Susan said.

"Do you remember the year we went up during spring vacation and got snowed in?" asked John.

"I'll never forget it," Father said.

"And Ervin and Bill rescued us with the truck and the snow plow," said David.

"And finally there was nothing left to eat, and for a whole day we just drank hot tea."

"And Father had to burn up all the furniture to keep the fire going."

"He didn't burn all of it," said Susan, who resented not having been taken along.

"Just *about* everything that would burn except for the bureaus," said Father. "Yes, I certainly remember that."

"Let's do it again next year," said John.

"Oh no you won't," said Mother.

"If we took Toast," John said, "we'd be safe. He'd get us out or bring food or find help or something."

"I really believe he would," said Mother. "But I don't want any of my family trapped in the snow again —especially without me there to take care of them. Living on tea, indeed! Do you think for a minute I'd have let you open up the cottage without putting in a good store of food?"

"Your mother's right," Father admitted. "We were very shortsighted. We didn't think beyond the good weather, we didn't check with our friends in Herbster about what we should prepare for, and we didn't take Mother *and* Toast."

"Can we use the *sauna* tonight?" Susan asked. She was still feeling a bit sorry for herself for having been left out of the great winter adventure. The thought of the Finnish bathhouse the Bark Point fishermen had built for them gave her a glow of comfort. Most of the settlers in that region came from Finland and they had brought with them the healthful and invigorating custom of taking steam baths, followed by a quick swim.

"I'd love to," Mother said, "but I'm not sure we'll have the energy to get the rocks heated and build the steam up. Maybe tomorrow."

"I gave a report in school about our *sauna,*" John said. "When I told them how cold Lake Superior is and how we jumped into it right out of the steam, the kids thought I was crazy."

"It's a scientific principle," David said. "The cold water closes the pores and stimulates the circulation. That's why you come out of the lake feeling warm."

"Absolutely correct," said Father.

"I wonder if John Roman will take us fishing on Siskwit, where the big sturgeon nearly pulled him to the bottom of the lake," David said. Now that everything was organized and seemed under control he was beginning to feel elated. Soon everyone was chiming in with his special "I wonder—" or "I remember—" or "I hope—" And Mr. Toast confirmed each happy recollection or expectation with a thump, thump, thump of his tail upon the floor of the car.

Toward noon Father turned off suddenly onto a country road. "Where are we going?" John asked.

"Aren't you getting hungry?" Father said, pulling off the road at a spot where some shady trees and a small brook seemed to invite them to stop.

Shouts from the other children approved Father's suggestion. Everyone got out of the car to stretch, and Mother spread a blanket on the ground for them to sit on around the heaping picnic basket she had prepared for them. All of them found it delightful to be munching sandwiches beside a country stream, with the possible exception of Toast. After eating a few scraps of roast beef, he began to pace between the car and his family, conveying a definite impression that somebody was wasting valuable time. He was a dog who loved the outdoors and on any other occasion would have romped beside the brook and across the fields, but today they had a mission. They were going to their own fields and woods. It was no time to dawdle.

"All right, Toast," Mother said finally. "We're as anxious to get there as you are. As soon as we've made everything tidy, we'll get back on the road again."

"All aboard!" said Father.

As the day became hotter the younger children grew restless. Much as he loved his brothers and sisters, David found it a bit wearing to be confined in the car with all of them for a long period. Some of the time being with your whole family was the most joyous thing in the world. But there were times when you needed to be by yourself, completely alone just to think. He felt Toast's muzzle on his knee, and his spirits improved immediately. Toast always seemed to understand how David felt.

He stroked Toast's head. In just another day they would be out together in the woods, in Toast's own territory. Everyone who knew Toast praised his keen intelligence, his sharp eye, and his unerring response to commands. These are characteristics of golden retrievers. Their specialty, of course, is to recover game shot by hunters, and a dog bred to be a hunting companion is expected to have all the abilities of a fine sportsman. Toast had them—and more. It annoyed David when people spoke of Toast as being "almost human." The most wonderful thing about Toast was that he was a superb animal—he was a *dog,* and as a dog he gave you something just a little different from what any human, even a member of your own family, could offer.

All at once there was a cry of anguish from Susan and a howl from Toast. The bird cage had come crashing down on Toast's head, and at the same time Susan came sprawling onto David's lap, nearly startling the wits out of him, for his mind was still in the north woods.

"Yow!" cried David, forgetting his adult manner completely.

"What happened?" Mother called back to them.

"Nothing," said Susan, scrambling to get to her feet and treading on both Toast and David in the process.

"What do you mean, nothing?" asked David, striving to regain his dignity.

"I was just checking to see if Brownie was all right," Susan said.

"Susan climbed up on top of everything and knocked the bird off," John announced.

"Eeeeeee!" Susan wailed and burst into tears.

"I don't see any serious damage," Mother said. "The bird seems fine."

"Good," said Father. "But unless everyone gets back into place and stays there still as a mouse, do you know what I am going to do? I am going to stop at the next town and leave everyone at the bus station and then I am going to drive up to Bark Point in peace and quiet."

"We'll be quiet and orderly," Mother said, as though she had been in some way responsible for the disturbance. "I'll tell you what—let's all play Ghost."

"All right." Father was willing to settle for anything within reason.

"Does everyone remember how to play?" Mother asked.

"I don't remember anything," Susan said hopelessly.

"It's a spelling game, but you can't spell," John told her.

"I can too," Susan said.

"Susan can play," Mother said. "Now listen carefully, so you'll know the rules. I say a letter. Then someone starts to make a word by adding a letter. Then the next person adds a letter, and so on around. Each letter has to build toward a word. If it doesn't seem to, the next person can challenge by asking what word you have in mind. If you can prove your point, the challenger has to drop out and then he's a ghost. If you can't, you drop out and you're a ghost. And you have to remember, the idea is to avoid being the one to *finish* a word. The person who does is out. The object, of course, is to stay in the game as long as possible."

"I've got a word," Susan said. "*D—a—l.* Doll."

"That isn't *quite* right," Mother said. "I forgot to say that the word has to have three or more letters to count."

"Oh," said Susan, not understanding at all.

"I'll start," said Father. "I'll start with *a.*"

"*B,*" said John.

"*C,*" said Susan.

"Challenge!" said Mother. "I can't form a word from *a—b—c.*"

"Then I won't play," said Susan.

"You can form *any* word from the *ABC*'s," said David wisely.

"Susan is right," Father said. *"ABC* is given in the dictionary as standing for the alphabet and also as meaning the rudiments of any subject."

"If Susan doesn't wreck the game, Father will," John complained.

"Susan is out anyway," Mother said. "She completed the word and it has three letters. However, I think I shall challenge John too. What word did you have in mind when you said *b?*"

"Abandon," said John.

"That's a good word," said Mother.

"But a sad one," said David.

"That all depends," said Father. "If I *abandon* you on the road, you will feel sad. But I shall then drive off with reckless *abandon,* feeling quite carefree."

"I suggest we play another game," Mother said. "Let's count the states we see on license plates."

As the day passed, even Toast adopted the air of one condemned to ages of silent suffering in close confinement. However, each stop at a gas station or at a wayside lunch counter provided a delicious reprieve. Everyone would come tumbling out and try his muscles, feeling as though years of being cooped up had made it unlikely that he would ever be able to move again. Toast bounded about like a puppy. The children jumped up and down. Father and Mother walked around and stretched and looked at their watches to see whether the trip was running on schedule. Then it was everybody back into the car, count noses, and off we go again!

By mid-afternoon, it was hard to tell who was sitting where. Everyone began shifting places with everyone else. Children were crawling over one another, Toast was crouching resignedly in his place on the floor, and Father was grimly intent upon following the road in its endless winding through the beautiful hills and thickening forests.

Finally, at a filling-station stop, Mother and Father had a conference over the road map. "Only one hundred miles to go," they said. "Last lap ahead!" And with this note of hope, everyone seemed to shake off tiredness and boredom.

The station attendants swarmed over the car, "filling 'er up," checking the oil, checking the tires. Then came the order to get on board, the usual confusion and shouting, and a final roll call, with each child answering by name. Then away they went, spirits lifted, and only a hundred miles to span!

Mother started a song, and soon they were all singing, even Baby Joe adding loud yaps and waving his arms.

The miles flew by on wings of song. And just as voices and energy were beginning to flag, the familiar landmarks began to appear and cries of recognition sped the travelers on. Only a few more bends of the road and the great lake would be shining through the trees. Soon they would arrive at the Point, looking across to the Apostle Islands, and beyond, unseen, the distant shores of Canada.

"There is Waino's strawberry field! And there's . . . ! And there's . . . and *here!*"

"We're *here!*" they shouted, as their own cottage came into view across a clover field. It was a little farmhouse near the shore, expanded with a wing here and there. Over the years new rooms had been added to house the growing family that occupied it each summer and adored it in memory through the fall and winter and the long, cold spring.

"Here we are!" As the station wagon drew to a stop,

everyone came piling out at once, out the doors and over the tail gate. Anyone watching at that moment would have seen only a blur of movement with figures jumping in every direction.

"Stop!" called Father. "Everybody take some luggage."

They began hauling their belongings into the house, Susan carrying the bird cage, the boys hoisting the heavy suitcases, Amy staggering along with a basket that was much heavier than it looked, Lisa with her two biggest dolls, Mother with Baby Joe under one arm and a roll of clothing under the other. Father stayed at the car, lifting out the remaining boxes and cases. The boys came back to help him carry them in.

When everything had been brought into the house, Father and the boys set to work opening the shutters while Mother and Susan made up the beds. After the most essential things were done, the family flocked to the kitchen to find what remained in the picnic basket for supper. Mother had made sure there was enough to see them through the day. After they had eaten a good meal of sandwiches, tomatoes, cookies and fruit, the older children scattered for a romp across the fields and a visit to the shore. Mother tucked Lisa and Baby Joe into bed and they uttered deep, happy sighs and closed their eyes.

Mother and Father decided that the rest of the unpacking could be attended to in the morning. They put a kettle of water on to boil for a pot of tea and went out on the porch and sat down together. They were not thinking about the miles that they had driven or the fact that they were very tired.

"I feel very peaceful," said Mother, looking out across the lake.

"So do I," said Father.

David had started out with the other children to revisit their familiar haunts. When they reached the woods, Susan stopped. She wanted to go to the beach, David wanted to strike out through the forest.

"Go along. I'll meet you all at the house," David said.

He plunged through a thicket and in a moment was out of sight of the other children. He knew his way and soon reached a path that led to a small clearing. Although the sun was down behind the trees, the open space was filled with light. It was just the time of day when you were most likely to see a deer appear as though by magic and stand in clear view amid the brush

and grasses. Toast was always the first to know when a wild animal approached and would freeze instantly in his tracks.

All at once David realized that there was no Mr. Toast at his side to give him the signal. "He went with the children," David thought. "No, he wasn't with us! He's off on his own."

If Toast was out exploring by himself, this was the place he was most likely to be. "Toast!" David called, forgetting his concern about disturbing the wild-life.

He heard sharp, crackling sounds from the under-brush, but no large golden dog emerged. Toast was not one to play hide and seek—David was sure of that. No doubt he was back at the house with the family, waiting for him.

Father and Mother were almost dozing on the quiet porch when David burst in.

"Dad," said David, "where's Toast?"

"I don't know," Father said. He was too content to notice the alarm in David's voice. "Isn't he with you?" he said.

"No," David said. "I can't find him."

"Find him?" said Father. "Well, go out and look for him. He must be with the other children."

"I was just thinking of sending Toast out to round up the children," Mother said as David started for the shore.

"And so we should," said Father. "I hope David brings him in."

After a time, David came back looking seriously upset. But he kept his voice low as he reported, "Dad, we can't find Toast anywhere."

Father didn't know whether to be alarmed or annoyed. As a result, he was both. "Bring in the other children," he said.

"All right." David was relieved that the matter was being taken out of his hands.

"What could possibly have happened to him?" Mother asked.

"To Toast?" said Father. "How could anything happen here to Toast? When did you see him last?"

"I just don't know," said Mother.

Within a few moments the children swarmed in, all looking as though they were practically bursting with important information.

Father waited for them to settle down, then he said,

"Now I want all of you to think carefully and tell me where you have seen Toast since we got here, and what he was doing."

John was the first to speak. "I saw Toast jump out of the car and run after something. I really did, Dad."

"Are you sure that's the *last* you saw of him?" said Father. He was still trying to come to grips with the fact that Toast had apparently disappeared. If a child had been missing, he would have been greatly concerned, but not surprised. But Toast! This was unheard-of.

"I'm sure," John said.

"Very sure?" said Father. He was saying to himself, "But Toast doesn't, *couldn't* disappear."

"Yes, Dad," John said. And his voice sounded strained. He was a truthful boy and it seemed strange for his father to be questioning him so very closely.

Father felt so sorry for John that he wanted to throw his arms around him and comfort him. But he knew that it was important for John to maintain his dignity in front of his older brother. So Father shifted the questioning to Susan.

"What about you, Susan?" he asked.

"I saw him, Daddy," Susan said. "He brushed my cheek with his tail."

"When we arrived here at the cottage?" Father said. "Are you sure of that?"

"Yes, Daddy," Susan said. "I'm sure."

Father had an unnerving moment of uncertainty. It occurred to him that whenever he had stopped the car along the road and got out, Toast had bounded out after him. But when the final stop was made, Toast had not done so. Father had *not* seen Toast upon their arrival at the cottage.

"David," Father said, "did you see him?"

"I'm not sure," David said. His doubts left him even more upset than John, but as the eldest child he felt his responsibility for controlling the situation. So he stood silently pondering: had he or hadn't he seen Toast? "Honestly, I'm not sure," he repeated.

"Well, the others saw him," Father said. "Did you see him, Amy?"

"Toast?" said Amy vaguely.

"What was Toast chasing?" said Father, returning to John. As he thought about it, it seemed to him that this was the crux of the problem. If Toast had not stayed with the family, there must have been a reason.

38

"Rabbit," said Amy.

Father wanted a reasonable explanation so badly that he did not pause to think he might possibly have put the word into Amy's mouth. "No wonder he's run off," he said. "All of you ran off, too. And it's been almost a year since Toast has had a rabbit to chase. Probably he's on his way back by now. Let's find him." Night was settling in, so he took the powerful electric torch and the family followed after him, shouting and whistling for their friend, Mr. Toast.

It seemed logical to try the lakeshore first. This was where Toast kept special watch over the younger children. This was where he had once dragged Amy out of the lake when Mother had left him in charge for a few minutes while she went to attend to something up at the cottage. This is where he had set out for a historic and successful two-mile swim in Lake Superior to join Father, who had neglected to take him aboard the boat for a fishing expedition.

But there was no Mr. Toast on the beach or running out of the brush in answer to the many voices calling for him.

"Do you know what I think?" said Mother.

Father admitted that he had no idea *what* to think.

"Keep calling up and down the beach," she told the children.

Then she took Father by the hand and led him back into the cottage. They went upstairs to their bedroom and Mother pointed to the bed. "Look underneath," she said.

It was an old brass bedstead with springs that groaned horribly and a mattress that sagged desperately in the middle. For years they had been saying they would buy a new bed, but had never got round to it. It was Toast's favorite hiding and sleeping place. Sometimes when Mother and Father had gone to bed, one of them would say, "Shall we go for a walk?" The other would say, "Yes, let's go for a walk." And then both of them would hardly be able to suppress their laughter at the sudden commotion taking place beneath the bed. It was poor Toast, pinned to the floor by the sagging springs, scratching for a foothold, gasping, grunting, heaving his seventy-five pounds of weight against the springs and mattress and finally almost tumbling his master and mistress out of the bed as he bounded forth, saying in manner if not in words, "Certainly, I'm ready to go for that walk!"

Now Father flashed the electric torch under the bed.

There was nothing to be seen but the bare floor and the sagging springs. No Mr. Toast.

All at once Mother and Father felt a wave of panic. For the first time they really believed that Mr. Toast was lost.

"I'm going to talk with the children again," Father

said, and started down the stairs, Mother following after him.

The children were already gathered on the porch. Their cries and their scouting up and down the shore had been fruitless. Now they stood huddled together, silent and heartsick.

David was thinking, "What's wrong with me that I don't even know whether Toast got out of the car with us at the end of the trip? Here I am, the oldest, and I seem to know the least about it of anyone. What am I, a 'stupe' or something? If he was with us, I should have seen him. If he wasn't, I should have known it. How could I let something like this happen?"

John was watching David's face, seeking some sign of comfort and hope and not finding it. "I can't understand it," he kept thinking. "If *I* saw Toast, why didn't David? *Everyone* saw him except David." And in his mind's eye, John saw Toast bounding across the lawn before the cottage, streaking off over the meadow and into the brush in hot pursuit of something. Seeing Toast so vividly in his imagination made him want to cry, but he only bit his lip and stood closer to David.

Susan held Amy's hand, feeling that the world had fallen to pieces and there was nothing to do but wait for someone to put it back together. When she saw Father and Mother coming she immediately felt re-assured.

"Susan," Father said gently, "think hard." He was terribly concerned about Toast, and at the same time he had a deep trust in his children. Susan was eight, and that is a pretty responsible age, but still, he did not want to upset her.

"Susan," he said. "Now, you did see Toast?"

"Yes."

"And his tail brushed your cheek?"

"Yes," she said, her voice unsteady.

"Show me just how," Father said.

"This way," said Susan, raising her hand to her face and running it slowly across her cheek.

She faced him squarely, a strong little figure, dressed in shorts and a white jersey sweater. Susan had jet-black hair and a fine, open face and the largest, most expressive eyes anyone has ever seen. When her Father looked at her, he knew that whatever Susan was saying, that was what Susan meant.

"You're quite sure that it was his tail that brushed your cheek?" he said.

"Yes," she said, "When he jumped out of the car."

43

"And can you remember anything else?" Father asked.

"No," said Susan, almost in tears.

Father put his arm around her. "Thank you, Susan. You've been a very good help," he said.

"But where *is* Toast?" said Susan, looking up at him.

"I don't know," said Father. "Never fear, though, we'll find him. Now go to bed."

Father took a turn up and down the porch looking out at the dark shore and the woods, then noticed that John was following close behind him. "John," Father said in a level, matter-of-fact voice. John was eleven, which is a *very* responsible age. "Are you sure that you saw Toast run after something?"

"Sure," said John. "You can ask Amy. She was standing right beside me."

"I have already asked Amy," Father said. "Where did he run?"

"Into the woods," John insisted.

Father gave John a "son, tell me everything" look.

"When the car stopped," John said, "we all got out fast and Toast pushed past me. I saw him run after something. Maybe it was a rabbit. Maybe a squirrel. But I did see him run toward the woods."

44

"You're quite sure?" Father said.

"Yes, Dad."

"Then let's get going."

On the porch steps, Father and John found David looking pensively into the darkness.

"What are you thinking?" asked Father.

"I just don't know," said David.

"Neither do I," said Father. "Come on."

They got into the car and began driving along the back roads.

Occasionally there were flashes of eyes from the brush or a small, furry creature scurrying across the roadway. "Toast knows this country better than we do," David said.

"He could be hurt," said John.

"If he can't make it himself, I'm afraid it will do no good to search until morning," Father said.

They turned back and drove toward the cottage. It was a clear, beautiful night, but the clean air and peaceful silence only added to their sense of loss and utter loneliness. It was good to see lights still blazing when they turned into the rutted lane leading to the cottage.

They came in the door and found Susan curled up in a chair, scarely able to keep from dozing.

"Where's Mother?" Father asked.

"She's on the telephone," Susan said.

"You go to bed," Father said. "Everyone go to bed."

Then he stalked off to find Mother and learn what was up. Poor Toast, he was thinking. If he could only talk, he would already have phoned *us*. Why didn't we ever think of *teaching* him?

"What are you doing?" he asked Mother.

"I'm trying to find Toast," she said.

"He can't talk," Father said, sitting down with a deep sigh. He felt tired and hopeless.

"I know," Mother said. "But I thought I'd call the police stations between here and our last stop. Somebody might have picked him up."

"He's such a gentleman," Father said. "Why would anyone turn him in to the cops?" He was so tired that he was feeling a little giddy.

"Of course," Mother said understandingly. "But I'm calling to make sure. So far, no results." And she consulted her road map to see where the next little town might be.

"I just don't know," said Father. "The children are so dead certain he was with us all along. I grilled them

46

like criminals. Even if I tortured them, they wouldn't change their stories."

"Well, don't do that," said Mother, smiling in spite of her distress. "Just try to think *where* we actually stopped last."

At first it seemed to Father that he couldn't think at all. Then it began to come clear to him. It was a gas station. He was sure of that. Together, he and Mother studied the map and decided upon the most likely location.

With his heart in his mouth, Father took up the phone and put in a call. It is wonderful what a long-distance operator can do for you on the basis of just a little information. Before many minutes had gone by, the station attendant was on the line.

Father explained the situation. He told the man he was sure they had stopped there in the late afternoon and they had had a big red dog with them, a dog about twenty-seven inches high, with a noble, intelligent face and a most dignified and respectful manner. The dog answered to the name of Toast, and had anybody seen him?

The attendant said he hadn't. He was the night man and had just come on duty. However, he was most

47

sympathetic and said he would get in touch with his partner and call back if there was anything to report.

Father gave him the telephone number and settled back to wait.

A half hour went by.

Perhaps there would be no return call. Perhaps their gentle friend and faithful protector of the household was gone forever. They might never know what had happened. How could they have left him behind? Could he have jumped or fallen out along the highway, unnoticed amid the confusion of children changing seats and crawling over one another? Or did he in fact leap out at the cottage door and vanish in a red flash down some magic rabbit hole?

"There are no magic rabbit holes around here," Mother said.

"I know," Father said. "Just deluded children."

Suddenly the phone rang.

Mother and Father sprang up, collided with each other, grabbed for the telephone, and got tangled up again.

"You take it," said Father. All at once he was afraid to answer it.

Mother said, "Hello," in a rather uncertain voice.

But then Father could tell from her expression that the news was good.

"There was a big red dog here, all right," the gas station attendant was saying. "My partner remembers seeing him, but he took off after a station wagon." Mother repeated his words for Father's benefit.

Father grabbed the telephone. "Listen," he said, "if that dog comes back, keep him there. Understand? And call us at once, regardless of the hour. There'll be a reward."

The man was obviously a dog lover and he understood perfectly. "I'll call," he said. "But you'd better get some sleep."

There was little sleep for Father. Poor Toast, he kept thinking. How we have betrayed you! He remembered the times when Toast had been in disgrace—usually for digging holes in the lawn. It was only necessary to say, "Did you do this?" and Toast would crawl to your feet, turn contritely onto his back, and stretch out his guilty neck as though to say, "Go ahead. Beat me. I deserve it." And at that point there was nothing to do but to get down on your knees and hug him, telling him that you loved him very much, but never, never do that again!

No one had ever really punished Toast or rebuked him with a harsh word. And now the whole family had not only lost him but probably broken his heart as well. Father could hardly stand it.

Both Father and Mother were up at dawn. Before he went down to breakfast, Father visited the children's rooms. Each child was sleeping peacefully. He thought of their awakening to find Toast still missing. He simply *had* to find Toast.

Father went into the room where David and John slept and sat down on the edge of David's bed. He shook David gently. David opened his eyes, shut them, then opened them again. "What is it, Dad?" he said.

"I'm driving back along the road to look for Toast," Father said. "Do you want to come with me?"

"Sure," said David, coming wide awake immediately and sitting up.

Father went over to John and shook him awake. When John saw his father's face, he broke into a happy smile. "Have you found him?" he asked.

"Not yet," Father said. "Do you want to come with David and me? We're driving back to look for him."

"Will we find him?" John said.

"I don't know," said Father. "Maybe he's around here instead. Do you want to stay home and look for him while we go out on the road?"

"I think he's around here," John said. "I'll stay and look."

"Fine," said Father, "but get some sleep first."

John buried his face in the pillow. Father waited until he was sure John had gone back to sleep before he left the room. David had already got his clothes on.

Mother had breakfast ready for them when they came downstairs. They ate quickly and silently. When they were through, Mother kissed them both and started them out the door. Just then the telephone rang.

"Your dog is here," said the man, calling from the gas station. "He must have come back after four a.m. when we closed up. He's just lying here at the office door. Won't budge. I tried feeding him, but he won't eat or drink. I think he'll stay here okay."

Father and David made a run for the car and hit the road. Mother waved wildly after them. Could it really be their Toast waiting for them a hundred miles away?

Now that they had positive word of a lost dog who might be Toast, both Father and David wondered why

51

they hadn't been *sure*. They hadn't definitely seen Toast arrive with them and they hadn't definitely *not* seen him. They simply took it for granted that he had been with them in the car for all those miles after he was already lost. No one had noticed. Father and David had believed Toast was with them just as strongly as Susan believed she felt his tail brush her cheek, as John believed he saw the red flash of Toast heading for the woods, as Amy believed she saw the rabbit that Toast was after. One way or another, every member of the family had seen a dog who wasn't there.

And meantime, far behind, the real animal, the true and loved Toast, must have been following along the highway in hopeless pursuit of the family he knew he had lost. When the sun went down, he had probably turned back and retraced his steps over the many miles to the exact point where they had left him. There he would wait, forever if necessary.

"He'll wait," David kept saying to himself.

"I'm sure he'll wait," Father kept hoping.

The country was hilly. Father was driving as fast as he dared. But he had to be careful, for it was impossible to tell what might be coming over the hilltop ahead.

Once he nearly hit a deer that emerged from the woods and flashed across his path. He slackened his speed, although his worry was mounting by the minute. After all, how would Toast know that Father and David were coming for him? *Would* he wait?

Ahead on the road they saw three bright red trucks, one behind the other. They seemed to be moving very slowly, for the Brents' car caught up with them quickly. They were piled high with gear, and Father and David saw by the signs on them that this was a traveling carnival. The trucks were so heavily loaded that it took all the power they could muster to get over each hill. Father's heart sank. He didn't see how he could ever get around them. Once he nosed the car out just enough to get a clear view for passing. But sure enough, over the hill ahead came another vehicle. Father dropped back into line hopelessly.

What could Toast be thinking? How hurt he must feel. To think that the whole family would go off and leave him, driving away with never a backward glance! Would he ever forgive them? Would he really be there when they arrived?

All at once the carnival trucks turned off on a little side road leading to a country town, where no doubt the village children were already waiting for the World of Fun Shows to arrive. David thought about Mother and the children back at the cottage and he guessed that they would not be in much of a carnival mood. Probably they were just now having breakfast. Mother would be telling them about the phone calls, and they would all be waiting anxiously for Father and him to return.

"What if Toast isn't there?" David said. "What if we don't come back with him? How can we break it to the family?"

Father was glad that David had dared to say it, for he too had been thinking about this terrible possibility. "David," Father said, "when it comes to the worst, all we can do is face it. But it helps to be able to face things together—that's one of the good things about being part of a family.

"Another thing to remember—if Toast never finds us or we never find Toast, someone else will surely find him and love him."

"He might even take up with the carnival," David said. "He might be a carnival dog." David didn't believe it for a minute, but it was better than imagining poor Toast wandering hungry and deserted along the roadways or through the fields, never again to find a familiar face or a beloved home.

All of a sudden Father put on the brakes with a tremendous screech. The gasoline station was just down the road!

Now that they were nearly there, Father was almost afraid to go on. Would Toast be there? And if he was, how would he act? Could they ever be friends again after such a betrayal?

"Go on, go on!" David kept saying. But Father drove very slowly the last few yards to the gas station. He inched along behind a car that was pulling in. He stopped the motor and opened the door and got out and started toward the office. David had already bounded out and was ahead of him.

Then they saw Toast!

Toast saw them!

They all leaped toward each other and collided in mid-air. The three of them went sprawling onto the gravel. Father tried to get up, but before he had managed it Toast was on top of him again in a wild embrace, and David was on top of Toast!

Finally, Father hung onto a gas pump while Toast planted his forelegs on Father's shoulders and David

tried to stretch his arms around the two of them. Toast was shaking with heartbreaking whimpers and Father and David were trying to say soft, soothing things while weeping at the same time.

A moment before, it had been just a normal morning at the gas station. Now motorists and station attendants were standing around watching a man and a grown boy and a large dog with their arms around each other's necks, sobbing and grinning and making the most extraordinary display of emotion ever seen on a quiet morning at a roadside filling station. Soon Father and David and Toast were encircled by the spectators, and some of them were crying too! To passing motorists, it must have looked like a small riot.

Finally father, son, and dog calmed down enough to follow the station manager into his office. Father telephoned Mother to tell her the good news, and the station manager told Father and David all that had happened down to the last detail.

The great mystery was: where had Toast been between four o'clock the previous afternoon and the following dawn? Traveling, apparently. He had started out in pursuit of the car and followed the road for hours and hours until he realized that it was all to no avail. Then he had decided to return to the place where the family had left him, reasoning perhaps, "If I can't find you, then you must find me. I'll go back to where you left me."

And back he came, setting up shop on the doorstep of the station, watching each car that came and went, but ignoring strangers and occasionally declining their attempts to pet him with a slight but meaningful baring of his long teeth.

He refused food or drink. He was deathly tired, but he remained alert, his head between his outstretched paws, looking, watching, waiting. He never barked. He scarcely moved. He just waited.

Father and David now thanked the station manager warmly and took Toast out to the car. Toast looked terribly done in. David examined his feet and found them sore and worn from his hours on the road. But what was worse was the look in Toast's eyes. They seemed swollen with sorrow.

Father understood how Toast felt. There had been experiences in Father's life that were just as bad. He knew what it was like. He knew that Toast would have to work it out for himself. But as they drove home to the cottage, Father talked to Toast quietly.

"Toast," he said, "nobody but you could have done it. I always knew you were brave, but I didn't realize how wise you are. You did just the right thing. Although it would have been perfectly proper for you to accept some water or eat the hamburger the man offered you. He was your friend, you know."

"It was all our fault," David said, patting Toast gently. "I'm terribly sorry. I was responsible, but toward the end of the trip I wasn't paying attention. You have no idea how much we missed you. And all the places we looked for you. And how we hurried back to get you. And how anxiously everyone is waiting for you right now. Please forgive us. We *really* thought you were with us all the time."

But Toast, sitting in the front seat between Father and David, was watching the roadway. The familiar landmarks were coming into view. *His* cottage and all the rest of *his* family were just ahead. He began pawing the seat of the car very softly, getting ready for the moment when they would turn down the lane to the cottage and their great reunion would be complete.

It *was* a great reunion, and after they had all hugged Toast and each other in an even more riotous version

of the gas station scene, they sat down outside the cottage to discuss the whole affair.

"But we were all telling the truth!" said John, grateful to have Toast back with them but deeply puzzled by the fact that Toast had *seemed* to be with them the whole trip.

"And yet it wasn't true at all," said David. David had *thought* Toast was with them. But he hadn't had visions. He couldn't *actually* have seen him when he wasn't there.

"No," said Father, "he wasn't here. That's the reality. When we come up against reality, our imaginings vanish into thinnest air. But you children saw it happen, and that's the truth."

"What's Daddy talking about?" Susan wanted to know.

"Your Daddy is getting all involved with very deep thoughts," Mother said. "It has to do with what people call illusion and reality. Pay no attention. At your age, all that is asked of you is to tell the truth as you see it. You told the truth. Love your dog and love your family and leave the rest to your parents."

"I nearly forgot Brownie, you know—" Susan began.

"Line up and count off!" Father said, as though suddenly shaken into action. "You, too, Mother. And you, Toast. You stay right here until I've counted everybody. I want to be sure for just one moment that I know what's what and who's where."

"Do you want me to get the bird?" Susan asked.

"Everybody stay just where you are!" Father commanded.

"Woof!" said Toast.

"I think I will teach you to talk," Father said to him.

"But he does talk," said Susan.

"Toast talks, Daddy," Amy said.

"All right, what's he saying?" Father said.

"He said he's going to chase a rabbit."

"Quiet now," Father said. "I really do want to count my family before we get under way with our summer. Where *is* that Toast?"

Everyone pointed to the woods.

"He went that way," said John.

"His tail brushed my leg," said Susan.

"He was after a rabbit," said Amy.

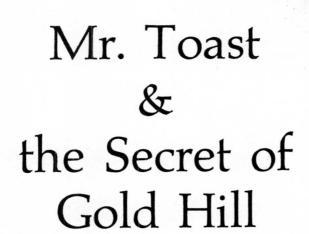

Mr. Toast
&
the Secret of
Gold Hill

by

Stuart Brent

Illustrated by George Porter

J. B. LIPPINCOTT COMPANY
Philadelphia   *New York*

For Ervin, my friend

Contents

Mr. Toast
&
the Secret of
Gold Hill

i

Toast Delivers a Letter

"The way I have it figured," John told David, "the treasure is buried right here."

John marked an X on the map, then lifted his pencil and began to retrace the route leading to this vital point. "Look," he said, "if the robbers pulled their sled over the lake ice, they would have come in toward Gold Hill from the little harbor where the fishing boats put in. We went in there with our boat when a squall blew up, remember? Probably there was a trail down to the shore just about where the map shows a road today. They could have followed that about three miles until they came to the hill.

"The contour lines on the map give you a pretty good idea how they could have made their way up around the side of the hill, and somewhere right near

11

here," he said, pointing with his pencil, "they would have found the going too tough. So they would have taken the trunk off the sled and either found a cave in which to hide the loot or dug a hole and buried it.

"Then," he continued, "they would have dragged the sled back to the main trail and left it there to throw everyone off the scent."

The topographic map before them was of the Bark Point, Wisconsin, area where the Brent family spent their summers. The map was filled with curving lines, each numbered in feet above sea level. A topographic map can be confusing until you become accustomed to it. However, with experience you are able to determine exactly where the hills and valleys are and where the country stretches out in level fields and plains. There are also symbols indicating trees or grassland or water.

John had become quite expert in reading such a map and could form an accurate picture of the country it represented. Father and the boys used the map when they went on fishing or hunting trips. It was a great help to be able to identify natural landmarks in country where the roads were mostly old logging trails instead of well-marked highways.

David studied the map and had to agree that the easiest way to go up Gold Hill would be along the winding path John had charted. "O.K.," he said. "When we go back to the Point, we'll ask Dad to take us over there so we can pick up the money."

"I know it's not that simple," John said. "But don't you think it would be a good idea to hunt for the treasure? It might really be there."

12

"Wonderful," David said. "But if I'm going to college in the fall, I'll probably have to work this summer."

Summer seemed far away, but John felt a pang of loneliness at the thought of leaving his brother behind when he went to Bark Point. On this rainy Saturday morning in early spring, he and David had shut themselves in their room and spread the map on a large drawing board. John was seated on the edge of his bed, working on the map, while David sprawled across the bunk above him, looking down at the map and the route John was charting. The pale gray and green rug beneath John's feet had been woven by Chippewa Indians at the Red Cliff Indian Reservation a few miles from Bark Point. Across the room on the wall above a chest of drawers hung a pair of deer antlers, a gift from Ervin, who ran the general store in Herbster, the nearest town to the Point.

It occurred to David that by the time another summer had come and gone, he would be leaving these familiar furnishings and keepsakes. He was just eighteen, and while he looked forward to going away to college, his mind was full of uncertainties. He wasn't sure what college life would be like or what he would choose to study. Sometimes he thought he would be a historian or a biologist, sometimes an engineer and sometimes an architect. John was a year younger than David and not yet face to face with these hard decisions.

David and John were occupying themselves with a game that in one form or another was a favorite pastime of all the members of the Brent family. It was the game of imagining they were up at Bark Point. Although they

13

lived comfortably in a large house in a suburb of Chicago, the place they loved best was their cottage in northern Wisconsin.

This country on the shores of Lake Superior was the land of their dreams in more ways than one. They dreamed about the fun they had in the fields and forests and on the water. They dreamed of their good friends who lived there the year round, like Ervin or the Indian boys from the Reservation who taught them archery. And they also enjoyed retelling the legends of frontier days in the North Country, stories their Bark Point neighbors told which had been passed along from one generation to another over camp fires and around the stove on winter evenings.

All of the old settlers at the Point had a supply of tales, but the best of all the storytellers was Wilbur Brookshaw. Whenever Wilbur stopped at the Brent cottage for an afternoon cup of tea, the children gathered around to hear his stories. They were always filled with excitement and suspense, and they all had the ring of absolute truth, although Wilbur warned them that a few of the facts may have become mixed with fiction.

No matter how fantastic the adventures were, every story Wilbur told was filled with exact details about the place where it occurred. Wilbur could always point out the precise landmark where each action took place: the rock near which a fisherman had encountered a sea monster in the lake, the meadow where a cabin stood that had been attacked by Indians, the wild strawberry patch where a little girl had been frightened by wolves.

14

The tale that David and John liked best was that of the wild escape into the Barrens of three bandits who, according to the story, had stolen $75,000 in gold from the government repository in Superior, Wisconsin. It was supposed to have happened in the late 1860's, although no one (least of all, Wilbur) ever seemed to have exact dates for the happenings they told about.

The Barrens is a strip of wilderness that lies about fifteen miles south of Bark Point and stretches west for several hundred miles into Minnesota. Unlike the treeless tundras of northern Canada, known as the Barren Lands, it is forested with birch and overgrown with dense underbrush. Beavers thrive along its streams and small lakes. There are deer and a few black bears and great numbers of smaller animals, including foxes and timber wolves. Although it is a woodland paradise for the nature lover, it is rough country and not a place to go without someone who knows it from long experience.

It was into this area that the gold thieves of Wilbur Brookshaw's tale disappeared with their booty. "How do you suppose they got away?" Wilbur had asked his listeners. "That gold was heavy and they had to move fast. There was an Army post at Duluth and as soon as word got to them, the whole company of soldiers set out with sleds and their teams of husky dogs to track down the robbers. Have you ever heard huskies baying in the night? That's a sound to frighten a stout-hearted man, to say nothing of a thief running for his life.

"Now, I'll tell you how the robbers made their getaway, just as my grandfather explained it," Wilbur said, lowering his voice as though he'd prefer the word didn't

15

get out. "It was the end of the winter, with the lake frozen solid hundreds of yards from the shore. So it wasn't hard for them to make good time pulling a sled across the ice.

"They had a head start—news didn't travel so fast in those days—so there was nothing to stop them as they came up the shore, past Bark Point and around the tip of our peninsula off the Apostle Islands and down toward Bayfield. They could have got away for sure into upper Michigan, then maybe gone inland over the ice along the Iron River to some hideout. They could have made it.

"Except . . ." Wilbur held up his hand dramatically. "Something happened they hadn't planned on. Overnight the weather changed and the spring rains broke loose. The lake ice was no longer safe. The robbers had to turn inland just below Bayfield and into the Barrens. They found a logging trail and at first they made some headway. But when the road got muddy, the sled bogged down.

"Anyone will tell you, three men can't get far in that kind of country lugging a heavy chest. The settlers who knew the Barrens joined the search. They found a sled abandoned on a trail near the foot of a hill. But nothing more. No robbers. No loot. No clue to where the treasure might have been hidden.

"But we know the gold is still there, somewhere. That's why we call it Gold Hill. A trunk full of gold just couldn't have been carried away through that kind of country in wet weather."

"Haven't you ever looked for it?" John had wanted to know.

"Plenty of folks have hunted," Wilbur said. "But that gold has stayed hidden for a hundred years and I don't think it's going to speak up and tell where it is."

John had made up his mind then and there to find out for himself if the secret of Gold Hill was as well hidden as Wilbur claimed. But the summer days had passed quickly and their vacation was over before he could talk Father into making a trip to explore the Barrens.

So on this rainy day at home, he and David were treasure hunting on the map, and John believed his reading of the map revealed where the treasure must have been left. All at once, they were interrupted by a thump at the door, followed by vigorous scratching. David jumped down from his bunk to open the door and was nearly knocked over as their dog Toast, a huge golden retriever, bounded in, tail wagging furiously and an envelope gripped in his mouth.

The boys were accustomed to Toast's delivering the newspaper in this manner, but it was a bit unusual for him to serve as mailman.

David took the envelope, which was addressed to Father and had already been opened. He pulled out the letter and read aloud:

"Weather has been very nice up here. The roads are very good. I am fine and am kept busy. Hope all of you are in the best of health and can come up this spring, as it is real early this year. If you have a spring vacation, this is the year to come. Your friend, Erv."

Of all the people they knew around Bark Point, Ervin had the greatest knowledge of the forests and lakes and was the most skilled in all the crafts a man needed to

17

master in order to live unassisted in that wild and beautiful country. An expert carpenter as well as woodsman, Ervin had helped Father and the boys build an addition to the Brent cottage the previous summer, for with the arrival of baby Joshua there were now eight children in the family. Since he was both a close friend and a man of few words, his invitation was not to be treated lightly.

John threw an arm around Toast, grabbed the letter in his free hand and waved it above his head.

"Hurrah!" he shouted. "We're going to do it this year! We're going up in the spring! Dad must really mean to do it or he wouldn't have sent Toast with the letter!"

"I'll bet he doesn't know we're going on a treasure hunt," said David.

ii

Toast Stops
an Argument

David and John, followed by Toast, came thundering
down the stairs to congratulate Father on his wise decision and tell what they thought would be the most exciting thing to do on a Bark Point spring vacation.

"Toast just brought us the news," John said breath-
lessly as they rushed into the study where Father was
reading the rest of the morning mail.

"Oh," Father said, without looking up. "I thought we
might run up there for a few days and do a little fishing.
Unless you fellows object, of course."

"Look at this," John said, spreading his map on
Father's desk. "David and I think we know where to
look for the Gold Hill treasure. Can we try to find it?"

"I hadn't quite bargained on exploring the Barrens,"

Father said. "We'd have to take camping equipment and . . . well, show me what you have in mind."

John repeated his explanation of how the formation of the hillside should give them a good idea of just how far three men could get with a heavy chest before having to stop to find a hiding place for it.

"Could be," Father said. "But I've never hiked around that part of the Barrens, so it's hard to say what we might be getting into."

"Erv would know the country," John said.

"I'm sure he does," Father said. "We could write and ask him what he thinks about it." Father's curiosity was becoming aroused.

"I suppose we could take the boat around there and hike inland. Then if nothing interesting turned up, we could go back and do some fishing. Well, don't get your hopes up too much. This may take some explaining to the rest of the family."

He got up from the desk and led the way to the living room, where Mother was reading by the fireplace and the younger children were engaged with rainy day occupations. Susan was sewing doll dresses for her sisters Amy and Lisa, who had set up housekeeping with their doll families. Adam was building a tower with blocks, while Joe watched with an expression of boredom, waiting for the structure to collapse. Baby Joshua lay asleep on a fur rug at Mother's feet.

"The boys and I are thinking of going up to Bark Point during spring vacation and hunting for gold," Father announced, breaking into the quiet atmosphere

21

of the room. Adam's tower fell with a crash. Everyone turned toward Father, and the expressions of excitement which he saw on the children's faces made him wish he had chosen a better way of saying that only he and the older boys were going.

"I can go," said Susan, dropping her sewing. "Can't I?" she added, her brown eyes suddenly looking much larger.

"We can't take girls into the Barrens," David said with authority. "This won't be a picnic."

"I'm big. I'm five," Joe said solemnly. At this, even David laughed, and Joe's eager expression changed instantly to one of such abject despair that Father quickly put his arm around him.

"If Joes goes, I can, too," said Lisa. "I'm much older." She was in fact a year older, but that meant she was in first grade, while Joe was only in kindergarten.

"Can I?" said Amy. While Susan, who was eleven, always showed her emotions at once, Amy, although three years younger, kept her feelings to herself except under grave stress. But once she set her mind on something, she would defy the full strength of the U. S. Marine Corps, politely but firmly.

"Go!" said Adam, now a sturdy three-year-old and determined to be a part of anything his brothers and sisters did.

Father didn't know what to say. He hadn't thought about anyone but David and John going with him. The fact that they were old enough to be completely self-reliant as well as good fishing companions was one of the reasons he had quickly decided to accept Erv's invitation. Until the gold business came up, he was only considering a short fishing trip anyway. It seemed much too complicated to take the whole family up there for just a few days. So Father stuck with his original decision.

"David and John will go with me," he said. "The rest of you will have to wait until you're a little older."

"How about me?" Mother said sweetly. "Am *I* old enough?"

Father didn't know whether to say that she was or that she wasn't, for she was looking at him with the same youthful excitement and expectation that he saw on the faces of the children. Maybe it was a poor idea all around, he thought, trying to check the boyish feelings in his own heart.

"I guess Mother is right," he said. "It wouldn't be fair to leave her with baby Joshua. Bark Point and Gold Hill and all the rest of it will keep until summer when there's lots of free time and we can all go."

"But it's spring vacation," Susan moaned.

"I won't be at Bark Point this summer. I'm planning to stay in Chicago and work," David said grimly.

"I want to go!" wailed Joe.

All at once, every voice was raised in argument or protest and Joshua, who had been sleeping soundly, awoke and burst into howls.

"It's David's fault," Susan said tearfully.

"It is not," David answered. "You heard what Father said."

Mr. Toast drew himself erect and uttered a low

23

growl. The confusion of voices ended abruptly. For Toast to growl was almost unheard of. He was the most gentlemanly of beasts, kind, polite, true, courageous, and so gentle that the smallest infant was safe in his care. There was only one thing he would not tolerate among his family, and that was an argument.

"Good boy," Father said. "This isn't the way to work out our problems. I'll tell you what. Mother and I will talk it over and see what can be done. Then we'll put the whole thing up to all of you. But until tomorrow, not another word. Right, Toast?"

Mr. Toast looked once around the assemblage, then walked slowly over to the fireplace and stretched out contentedly on the floor.

The whole family found it hard to be patient while waiting to learn what the decision would be.

"I think it's all off," David told John that night as they were getting ready for bed. "I'm sure Dad wants to go, but he can't hurt everyone's feelings by taking just the two of us."

"That's the trouble with a big family," John said. "Who ever heard of a family of *eight* children? I don't see how we ever get to do anything."

"Large families are a little unusual these days," David admitted. "They're not popular."

"I can see why," John said.

"Well, if you wanted to cut down the size of our family, where would you start?" David asked.

"Forget it," said John. "Forget the whole thing."

Susan, however, was sure they were going. "You'd

better decide what you want to take with you," she told Amy in whispered tones, so as not to wake Lisa.

"I don't think we can go unless Mother does," Amy said.

"If you ask me, Mother is going," Susan said with calm assurance. Susan had a tendency to break into tears easily, but when faced with emergencies or important issues, she was steady as a rock.

In the meantime, Mother and Father, after looking in at Joe and Adam and Joshua, all of whom were sleeping soundly, sat down by the fireplace to talk thing over.

"Why don't you and the boys go up there?" Mother said. "I can find enough things to keep the rest occupied while you're away. You deserve a vacation, you know, and it will be good for John and David. They won't have many chances to do things together when David goes to college."

"I have a better idea," Father said. "I think we should *all* go."

"But it's such a long trip for a week's vacation," Mother said. "It was the way you announced it that got everyone so excited. As though gold had been discovered and we should start right out and get some. You know about gold fever—"

"You haven't heard the whole idea," Father interrupted. "David and John and I can drive up with all the gear we need, and the rest of you can fly."

"I never thought of that," Mother said. "The children would love it. So would I."

"Then it's settled," Father said.

25

Toast lifted his head, then sat up.

"Come on, Toast," Father said. "It's bedtime for everyone.

"You never know what to expect of parents, do you?" David commented to John after they had learned the new plans.

"I think it will work out just fine," John said. "You and I can drive, so it won't be a hard trip for Dad. And Susan's old enough to give Mother a hand with the kids."

"Can I go in the car?" Joe asked. He was perched atop John and David's bunk beds, listening intently to their conversation.

"Wouldn't you rather take the airplane ride?" David said.

"I suppose so," Joe said, but he didn't sound entirely convinced. In spite of the difference between his age and theirs, Joe had a close association with his older brothers. He shared a bedroom with them up at the cottage, and from the time he was a toddler had more often than not taken part in their games and shared their interests. Usually they enjoyed having him with them, but sometimes they arranged to get away before Joe knew about it. Joe learned that a good way to avoid being left out was to keep his ears open.

"Don't worry," John told him. "It's been decided definitely that everyone is going. It doesn't matter how you travel."

"I'll fly," Joe said, and making a great whirring sound

26

spread his arms and leaped off the bunk onto David's shoulders.

For John, the best news was that Ervin approved of a trip to the Barrens. Their friend responded to Father's

letter with a postcard that said: "O.K. to go camping down at Gold Hill. Florence says maybe she will cook for us." Ervin's wife, Florence, was renowned for her ability to turn out great meals over a camp fire.

Father, David, John, and Toast departed by car, according to plan, a day ahead of the rest of the family. The younger children all stood at the front window watching the loading of the car with piles of blankets and bedrolls and what appeared to be enough heavy clothing to outfit an expedition to the North Pole. Toast kept running back to the house to bark at them, as though to assure them that they would be in good hands until they saw him again.

Early the next morning, Mother piled the rest of the family into the station wagon and drove out to the airport. She would leave the car in the airport parking lot until their return. The day was gray and drizzly and a raw wind was blowing. Although everyone was excited, nobody talked very much. If the weather were like this in Bark Point, Mother thought, they might have to spend the whole week in the cottage.

"Ervin promised the weather would be good," Susan said.

"Of course it will be," Mother said.

Once inside the air terminal, the children forgot their worries about the rainy day. Long corridors stretched in a confusing number of directions. Everyone bunched closely together and followed Mother to the counter where they checked in the small amount of baggage they were carrying and were told where to go to board their plane.

Off they went down a hall that seemed to go on forever. On either side were waiting rooms with large windows through which they saw enormous airplanes.

"Are we going on one of those?" Joe wanted to know.

28

"We won't be taking a big jet plane," Mother said. "But our plane will be lots of fun. Wait until you see it."

They kept on walking until they were nearly at the end of the concourse. "Here we are," Mother said. She showed their tickets to a man in an airline uniform and took the children over to the window. Down below them stood an airplane which, although a good bit smaller than those they had first seen, looked as though it could hold the entire Brent family and a considerable number of other people as well.

"That's called a DC-3," Mother said, "and when I first traveled by airplane, nearly all of the passenger planes were very much like it. We used to think they were huge. It's still a very good airplane for use when you do not have too far to go."

"But it's a long way to Bark Point," said Amy.

"Not when you fly," Mother said.

iii

On the Water

Ervin and Toast met the plane in Duluth. When Mother and the children came down the steps off the plane, Toast was first in line to greet them, standing with his forepaws on the fence near the arrival gate.

They all piled into Ervin's car and drove to Bark Point, where Father and David and John were busy getting everything ready for their expedition. Ervin had been right about the weather. It was a beautiful sunny day in Bark Point. Father and the boys had opened all the doors and windows of the cottage, letting in the warm sunshine and the soft breeze from the lake. There was not a fly or gnat or mosquito to be seen. It was perfect.

Down the beach and across the lake, as far as the eye could see, there was not a boat or a human being, not even the trail of smoke marking the course of an ore ship. There was just the lake and the shore and the tall birches and evergreen and the whispering of the south wind.

As soon as the luggage was put away, the children scattered. Susan was off to look for rocks and shells to add to her collection. Amy scampered off to a secret cranny where she remembered hiding something last summer. A moment later she uttered a cry of delight, "My doll!"—and was heard no more.

Adam solemnly marched off to the beach with bucket and shovel to play in the sand. Although only three, he could be trusted to stay at a safe distance from the edge of the water. Joshua headed for the pantry and began taking the pots and pans from the shelves and arranging them across the floor. Mother didn't mind in the least. It seemed much easier to put things back in order again at the cottage than at home, and her helpers were always more willing.

Joe, with Toast at his heels, set out to look for John and David, who had disappeared soon after the family's arrival. It didn't take long to find them down in the boathouse.

"Here comes trouble," John warned David, looking out the doorway and observing Joe's approach.

"He's all right," David said. "He's our brother, you know."

"With the whole gang up here, something is bound to go wrong," John said. "Someone will get lost or hurt and we'll spend all our time rushing around and never get started for Gold Hill."

"Hi, Joe," David called, as Joe and Toast came charging in. "Give a hand here and help us with the fishing gear. If you do a good job, maybe we'll take you for a boat ride."

Back at the cottage, Father was busy assembling the camping equipment. He came out into the kitchen carrying a rolled sleeping bag and crashed into Joshua's stockade of cooking pots.

"Keep your feet out of the frying pans!" Mother said gaily. "Better still, sit down and have a cup of coffee."

"I think I will," Father said, putting down the bedroll.

"The house smells so fresh," Mother said. "You wouldn't know it had been closed all winter."

"Everything seems to be in good working order," Father said. "Although we lost the canned goods in the pantry."

"What happened to them?" Mother asked.

"They burst," Father said, laughing. "We didn't have sense enough to realize that the cottage gets freezing cold in the winter."

"And I thought we could try the strawberry jam I put up last summer," Mother said, shaking her head.

"Had to throw it all out," Father said. "Never mind. Erv and I put in supplies before he drove out to get you. And in the refrigerator there's even a pail of smelt that we caught this morning."

Mother and Father walked out on the porch and looked across the water, sparkling in the spring sunlight.

"The trouble with coming up for a week," Father said, "is that it makes me want to live here forever."

"I know," Mother said, understandingly. "Well, how are the plans for the expedition coming along? So far as that goes, *what* are they?"

"The fastest way to get where we're going is to drive, if you know the roads," Father said. "This famous hill lies just about forty miles straight across the peninsula. But I like the idea of taking the boat around. Erv says most of the ice is out, so it should be safe. It's probably about a six-hour trip and there are plenty of good places to put in if the weather turns bad. We'll start in the morning, and Erv will leave in his jeep later in the day and drive across to meet us."

"Do you really expect to find anything?" Mother asked.

"Not likely," Father said. "But when we get tired of hiking, we can always go fishing."

"Are we going tomorrow?" Joe asked. He had come onto the porch so quietly that Mother and Father both jumped at his voice.

"You're not," Mother said. "Not tomorrow. Some year when you're older."

"I'll be six years old," Joe said. When you are five years old, it seems as though you'll be very much older when you are six.

"Joe's a good fisherman," Father said thoughtfully. "He's patient and he always obeys instructions. Once we get there, we'll be doing most of our traveling in the jeep, so the hikes won't be too long. Besides, Toast would keep an eye on him. I'll tell you what. If the weather's good tomorrow when we start out, Joe may come along."

"Then I'd better get ready," Joe said earnestly, and left the porch.

A moment later, David and John came up the path from the boathouse with Toast following closely behind them.

"We'll have to pack some additional grub and gear," Father told them. "Joe's coming along with us."

"We're taking *Joe?*" John said in disbelief.

"Sure you are," Mother said. "He isn't a baby and besides, he'll bring you luck."

"I hope Mother's right on both counts," David said.

John nodded, but his expression said, "Didn't I tell you?"

Toast woke David and John before dawn. David's first impulse was to push Toast away. He thought he had been asleep for only a short time and that the hour must be around midnight. But the sound of voices in the kitchen and the smell of fresh coffee suggested that this was not the case. David sat up, patted Toast on the head, and shook John, who had responded to Toast's pawing by burying his head under the pillow. Joe's cot, David noted in the faint light, was empty. The room was cold and it took a bit of courage to leap out of bed, but in a moment both David and John were on their feet and, wrapping their bathrobes around them, they followed Toast into the kitchen.

Father and Joe were sitting at the table and Ervin stood by the stove, drinking a cup of coffee and urging

Father to set a course that would keep the boat in sight of shore. There were still numbers of ice floes on the lake, and Ervin was not one to let his friends take unnecessary chances.

"I'll help you load your supplies on," Ervin offered.

"No, you go on ahead," Father said. "I have plenty of deckhands." He knew that Ervin had to get to Herbster to open his store and see that the day's business was well in hand before leaving his assistant in charge and setting out in the jeep.

"O.K., see you this afternoon," Ervin said, setting down his coffee cup.

"Don't get lost driving through the Barrens," Father said.

"I never get lost," said Ervin. Everyone laughed, for they all knew the story of Ervin and Father getting lost years before while hunting in the Barrens. They had a compass, but Ervin, who thought he knew the country perfectly, refused to believe that the compass needle was pointing properly. As night came on, they heard noises that seemed to be getting closer and they began to run. As they ran, the sound continued to pursue them, a sort of soft, persistent thumping. It was a terrifying sound of a kind they had never heard before. Finally they stopped short to gather their wits and all at once realized what it was. They were being pursued by nothing but fear, for the sounds they had been hearing were their own heartbeats!

Having waved good-bye to Ervin, Father and the boys finished dressing and went down to the boat house to wheel the boat out and draw it up alongside the dock. It was a fine boat, twenty feet long, and out on the water it always handled splendidly, cutting into the waves and staying as dry as could be. Driven by a powerful seventy-five-horsepower motor, it made up to twenty miles an hour, which is a pretty good speed on the water, and it could be depended upon to cruise along at about four-teen miles an hour even when heavily loaded.

By the time Father had connected the motor and the boys had loaded on the tool kit, the extra cans of gaso-line, the compass, the paddles, the life preservers, and the small extra motor (carried along in case of emer-gency), the sky had brightened and up in the cottage the rest of the family were stirring. While Mother prepared breakfast, Susan gave the boys a hand carrying the knap-sacks, sleeping bags, digging instruments, food, and fishing equipment to the dock and loading them aboard.

"If you see any unusual rocks, will you pick them up for me?" she asked John. He promised that he would.

It took but a few minutes for Father and the boys to eat breakfast and get ready to shove off. By now the younger members of the family were up and dressed. Mother and Susan brought them all down to the shore to witness the departure.

The members of the expedition took their positions. David stationed himself on one side of the boat ready to paddle it toward the deep water. John sat at the stern next to the motor, prepared to lower the propeller into the water. He found the sight of the group waving to them from the shore less than thrilling. "Honestly," he said to David, "you'd think we were sailing for Antarc-tica."

Mr. Toast, however, returned the calls and hand-waving of their wellwishers with hearty barks and rapid flourishes of his tail. Toast stood in the middle of the boat, while Joe sat in the bow with Father by the controls.

"Cast off," Father said.

David plied his paddle and the boat swung out away from the dock. John released the spring that held the motor in lifted position and the propeller swung down into the water. Father glanced back to see that all was in order, then pressed the starter. He held the motor running in neutral for ten seconds, then gently pushed the throttle to forward position. They were off!

"It's going to be a fine day!" Father said. But the scene looked gray and cold as they cut out into the open waters of Lake Superior, heading northeast toward Sand Island. It was for good reason that the fisherman of Bark Point called Superior "the ocean." Its size, the great depth of its waters, and the violence of its storms command the respect of those who travel it.

As they started out, there was a cold spot in the pit of David's stomach that had nothing to do with the raw wind or the fact that he had barely touched his breakfast. He had sailed the lake ever since he was a small boy, but this morning everything seemed different. He had the crazy notion that he was leaving for somewhere unknown and might never again see the members of the family left on the shore behind them. It was all imagination, and he knew it, but he still felt that cold spot.

Don't panic, he said to himself. Relax and enjoy the trip.

"May I have something to eat?" Joe asked. It was the first word he had spoken since they got on board. David looked at the small, bundled figure and the eager face beneath the stocking cap pulled down over the ears. All at once the cold spot in David's stomach disappeared. With a laugh he began hunting among the supplies for bread and sausage.

Toast stood up and made his way carefully to the bow of the craft where Father and Joe sat at the controls. Toast nuzzled them gently and curled up on the seat between them. David was amidships preparing sandwiches and John sat at the stern watching the wake of the boat cascade behind them in the sunshine. It had become a brilliantly clear day. The lake was smooth and John could see the boat's shadow gliding over the water alongside them. It was cold out on the water, but John was wearing his fur-lined parka and felt warm and full of joyous excitement. They had passed Sand Island and, rounding the point of the peninsula, turned to the south. To their left were the Apostle Islands, a chain of innumerable islands, large and small, their gray rocky banks and wooded slopes clearly defined against the deep blue of the water and the light blue sky. There is something about an island that arouses curiosity. It would be fun someday to explore the Apostles, John thought. But the shoreline at his right attracted his interest even more, for with a bit of imagination he could visualize the route he believed to have been taken by the gold thieves in their trek over the ice off the shores of the mainland.

The first two hours of the trip passed uneventfully.

Here and there Father had to dodge floating masses of ice, but for the most part it was clear sailing and with the shoreline always in view it was no trouble to stay on course. Then quite suddenly the sun was clouded over and they found themselves moving into thickening fog.

"David, you'd better join me here in front," Father said. "This may be interesting."

By the time David had made his way to the bow, Father had cut the speed of the boat to half and stowed Joe in the storage space under the forward deck, which provided a cozy shelter.

"Where did all of this come from?" David asked. "A minute ago there wasn't a cloud in the sky."

"All it takes is a change in the air currents," Father said.

The fog closed in around them. From the stern, John could see Father and David and Toast only as shadowy forms. He wondered whether this expedition he'd been so keen about was such a good idea. They had never sailed the lake this early in the year. John could feel his heart pounding and thought of the story about his father and Ervin getting lost in the Barrens. "Well, anyway," he thought, "I know there's nobody chasing us. They couldn't see us if they were!"

"We are simply sailing through a low bank of fog," Father announced calmly. "Just above this fog, the sky is as clear as ever. We'll soon be out of it, but meantime you'd better light a flare."

As David started rummaging in the supply locker, there was a sudden tremendous roar just off their starboard side. David staggered to his feet and lit the flare.

They could see the ghostly forms of two ice floes which had collided and were grinding into each other with the most fearsome racket.

Father throttled the motor down to trolling speed and the boat glided safely past the two ice monsters. "Whew!" he said. "That was a close one!"

"Watch out for more of them," David said. "Shall I get a paddle to fend them off?"

But now the fog was lifting, and with surprising suddenness they sailed out into bright sunlight and dancing blue water.

Joe poked his head from the storage space. "Can I come out now?" he asked.

It was high noon, and in spite of the cold wind they could feel the warmth of the sun. They loosened their heavy garments and set to work preparing lunch: bologna and cheese sandwiches spread with mustard, hot cocoa from the Thermos jug, and cookies and candy bars for dessert. Everyone felt relaxed, content, and encouraged by the knowledge that more than half the voyage was safely behind them.

As the afternoon wore on, Joe crawled back into the storage space to nap and David and John took turns with the binoculars trying to spot the harbor entrance near *Gold Hill*. Although it was still brilliantly clear over the lake, the shoreline was shrouded and the hill toward which they set their course was indistinct. Once in a while the low clouds that veiled the top of the distant hill parted and something gleamed like burnished metal.

41

"Look," John called out, "there's the gold!"

"Could it really be gold?" David asked.

"No," Father said. "I don't think the treasure is spread out on the hill top. That reflection must come from crystals in the rocks. But I am certainly anxious to take a closer look."

"So am I," said John.

Soon the smell of fog was in the air again. Its damp breath filled their lungs. If the fog closed in on them again, David did not see how they could possibly find the harbor.

Within a few minutes the haze thickened and the fog that had obscured the shore settled down upon them like piles of white cotton, blotting everything from view. Father reduced their speed again. "Get out the foghorn," he told David, "and start sounding it about every two minutes. We're headed toward shore and there may have been boats behind those fog banks."

David rummaged about in the supply chest. "It isn't here," he said finally.

"And I thought I had checked everything so carefully!" Father said. "Well, if we see or hear anything coming our way, we'll just have to yell at it."

"Is our old compass reliable?" David said.

"Now you ask!" Father laughed. "It had better be. It's all we have to guide us."

For what seemed like an eternity, they crawled forward. Father turned on the headlight that was mounted on the bow, but it only glowed in a sickly way that made the dense fog seem spookier.

"Shall I light another flare?" David said.

"No use," Father said.

All at once, they were startled by the hoarse cry of a horn braying across the water. Peering through the glasses in the direction of the sound, David could not detect even the shadow of another boat. He was still gazing blindly when Toast pushed him aside and leaped up on the prow. Lifting his head, Toast emitted a baleful howl that David and John were sure could be heard all the way to Bark Point. Immediately there was an answering blast, louder than the first. Somewhere out there a boat was headed toward them.

"At least this is better than the ice floes," Father said hopefully. "They don't blow their horns to warn you off."

Father shifted their course a little, while Toast continued to bay. The next blast from out of the fog did not sound quite as strong. Then, as before, without any warning, the fog lifted and as though by magic the shape of a fishing boat appeared a few hundred yards away. It was a fair-sized craft, sturdily built for rugged work on the Great Lakes in all kinds of weather.

Toast answered the blast of the boat's horn with a triumphant bark. Then Joe piped up, "I hear a bell!"

Father took the glasses and scanned the water. "I can see the first buoy," he said. "We're headed straight for the harbor."

"Who's ringing the bell?" Joe asked.

"It's a floating bell. The water rings it," Father said. "It's ringing to tell us that we're safe."

"Hey," John said, "the fishing boat has swung around."

45

"Sure enough," Father said. "It's going to guide us through the channel. All we have to do now is follow."

"How about some coffee, Dad?" David asked.

"Fine," Father said. "And for goodness sakes, give Toast a snack. I hate to think what might have happened if he weren't in such fine voice."

David gave Toast a dog biscuit. Then he got the Thermos and served his Father a cup before filling a tin cup for himself. He suddenly realized that his teeth were chattering. He felt proud of Toast and of his father's seamanship, but somehow, as they sailed into the channel, he felt melancholy. Perhaps it was because all color seemed now to be drained from the sky and water, leaving only shades of gray. Perhaps it was the combination of elemental, lonesome sounds: the swishing of the waves, the screech of the seagulls, the mournful tolling of the bell buoy rocking in the waves.

Impulsively he turned toward little Joe and gave him a firm hug. "Mother was right," he announced. "Joe brought us luck."

John grinned. "Yeah," he said, "everything is turning out fine."

iv

The Fight

They tied the boat securely to a weatherbeaten wharf. Toast bounded out and was first ashore. David reached down to give Joe a hand, for the pier stood high out of the water, its massive piles supporting a platform of rough timber. It dated back to the days when the harbor was a base for many fishing boats. Once there had been a small village here, but the town and the fishing fleet had disappeared. The younger people had gone to work in Superior or Duluth or Saint Paul, where they could make better money. The villagers who remained found the Lake trout becoming scarce because of the lamprey eels, which appeared in great numbers and attacked and destroyed the fish. By the time ways had been found to subdue the eels, the village was deserted. Now only a few boarded-up buildings remained, along with broken-down racks for the drying of nets, fragments of machinery, and skeletons of abandoned boats. Only the pier was kept in a rough state of repair by the few fishermen who still put into the harbor and who lived inland along the old logging roads.

The fishing boat that had guided them through the channel did not tie up at the pier. Instead, after an exchange of shouted greetings between the three members of its crew and the Brents ("Want to sell that meat-eating foghorn?" the captain asked), the boat swung around and headed out toward the open water, the fog banks and the ice floes, and the hope of getting another haul of trout or whitefish before putting into port farther up the coast.

The wind had freshened and the lake looked gray and choppy. Father wished he could beach their boat, but that would have to wait until Ervin arrived with the winch and heavy chain that were part of the jeep's equipment. Although the boat was securely tied and protected by the pier, Father was afraid some of the ice floes might wash into the channel and crush their small vessel. Well, there was nothing to do, he guessed, but to wait for Ervin to show up. Meantime, in the few hours remaining before sundown, they could unpack their gear and find a camping place.

They all set off to explore the area. The spring thaws had come early and the ground was spongy beneath their boots. "I hope Ervin hasn't got stuck somewhere," John said. Now that they had actually arrived at the place he had been dreaming of, he didn't want anything to go wrong.

About a thousand feet inland and up the slope from the shore, Father found a good dry spot to pitch their tent. They stretched the canvas on the ground. Joe helped out in placing the stakes correctly and even took a hand at driving them into the ground with the hammer. Once the tent poles were raised beneath the canvas and the ropes pulled taut, it was an admirable shelter.

While Father and John went back to the shore to get sleeping bags and blankets, Joe helped David dig a shallow trench around the outside of the tent. In case of rain, this would catch the water and keep the ground dry inside the tent. By the time the sun began to set behind Gold Hill, all of their equipment had been carried up to the camping site and Joe was happily rolling about on an air mattress inside the tent and wanting to know when they could all crawl into their sleeping bags.

"Unless someone wants to go to bed hungry," Father said, "I'll need all hands to help with supper."

Night came on swiftly. David and John soon had a good fire going. They all crouched around the blaze and waited for the flames to subside a bit before Father started the hamburgers and fried potatoes.

"Ummm," said Joe, as Father began to turn the hamburgers on the grill with his long cooking fork. "I can't wait!" There is nothing quite like the smell of food cooking in the open air to whet the appetite.

"Get your plates ready. Hey, don't push me into the fire!" Father said, as the boys and Toast crowded around him. "Give me Toast's plate, too," he added, and served a generous amount of raw ground meat for the dog.

49

All was silent except for the snapping of jaws, and in what seemed to be no time at all everyone had devoured his first helping.

"You'd think none of us had ever seen food before," Father said, as he ladled out spoonfuls of creamed corn that he had heated in a can over the coals. "Go ahead, finish it up. You'll need strength tomorrow."

When they had sipped their hot cocoa and watched the fire die down, Father and Joe turned in. David and John stayed outside the tent with Toast, watching the embers glow and wondering what had happened to Ervin.

"If Ervin doesn't show up, we've got a long hike ahead of us," John said. "What will we do about Joe?"

"If he gets tired, I'll carry him," David said.

"Not far, I'll bet," John grumbled.

Toast stretched himself out beside the fire, his powerful body, unusually large for a golden retriever, glowing a deep golden brown in the firelight. He weighed all of ninety-seven pounds and was truly magnificent to look at. Somehow Toast by the camp fire was a different creature from Toast sitting by the fireplace at home. At home he was polite and loving and highly responsible, a truly civilized dog. But out here in the wilderness, he seemed to gain added authority. Even as he dozed by the fire, he held his nose tilted upward, as though he were keeping in touch with the mysteries and possible dangers of the forest. He understood this country. He was in charge.

David and John sat for a long time in silence. Finally

David said, "Do you know, I was really scared out there on the water."

"If you think you were the only one, forget it," John said. "Those ice floes in the fog got me. Especially when Dad cut the motor and we just drifted. I had an oar ready to try to push the ice away if it hit us, but I don't think that would have worked. One hit and the boat would have been crushed."

"I guess the sea is for sailors," David said. "I'll take dry land. At least it gives you something to hold onto. You sure feel small out there."

"Well, we're not very big up here in the Barrens," John said. "Even Ervin seems to have got himself lost."

"If he's lost, he'll get un-lost," David said confidently.

"Sure," John said. "Let's turn in."

"Go ahead," David said. "I'll fix the fire."

David banked the fire carefully by raking ashes over the coals. This would keep the flames from spreading in case a wind came up, but the embers would remain glowing and alive to rekindle the fire in the morning.

He took a last look around, and everything seemed secure. David started toward the tent and Toast got up and followed him. David turned and took Toast's noble head between his hands. Toast closed his eyes, laid his ears flat against his head, and tried to nuzzle deeper into David's arms.

"Good night," David whispered, and crawled into the tent. He crept into the corner where he had placed his sleeping bag, removed his shoes and trousers, and managed to work himself into the bag without disturb-

51

ing the others, who were sleeping soundly. He zipped the bag up to his chin, turned once or twice to make himself comfortable, and was quickly asleep. Outside, Toast stationed himself in front of the tent opening.

David did not know what awakened him or how long he had been asleep. He sat up alert and listening. At first there was nothing but the usual forest sounds, the wind blowing through the pines. Then he heard a low, menacing growl, deep and ugly.

David waited a minute. The sound was repeated. He nudged John. "Toast's growling," he whispered.

John stuck an arm out of his sleeping bag and propped himself up on his elbow. "I don't hear anything," he said in a sleepy, complaining voice.

At this there was a loud baying followed by a hysterical, high-pitched howl. In a moment everyone in the tent but Joe was awake and struggling into shoes and trousers, bumping into one another in the darkness, and all but knocking the tent down.

Once outside the tent, they paused to get their bearings, then began running, Father in the lead, in the direction of the sounds. About fifty yards from the camp they came in sight of Toast circling a slightly larger animal with pointed ears and spindly legs.

"Toast! Toast!" David shouted. But Toast, teeth bared and lower lip drawn back, paid no attention.

"It's a timber wolf!" Father called. "Throw things at him while I try to get Toast!" He tried to keep his instructions calm, but he was actually yelling at the top of his voice.

As Toast circled the wolf, Father approached cautiously with his hunting knife drawn. At the same time, David and John began hurling stones and whatever sticks or dead branches they could get their hands on. They might as well have saved their energy: neither animal gave them the slightest heed.

Father shouted again in the hope of attracting Toast, and at that moment the wolf lunged. Toast caught the full impact of the leap against his chest, and both animals went down in a snarling heap.

Father stopped short. There was nothing he could do to cope with this howling mass of fury. Then an idea struck him. "Get some blankets!" he called. David and John dashed off toward the tent and were back in short order with two blankets. He'll be killed, John was thinking as they ran. That wolf will kill Toast and Dad can't do a thing about it.

By the time the boys were back, the animals had separated and were stalking each other for the next round. Father seized a blanket, stretched it out between his arms, and leaped into the battle like an insane bullfighter.

For the first time, the animals appeared to notice that intruders were present. Father rushed at the wolf and tossed the blanket, hoping to trap the beast beneath it for at least long enough to catch Toast. But the wolf sidestepped neatly and bore in again on the dog. This time Toast dodged the full brunt of the attack and drove his body against the side of his adversary. The wolf reared onto his back feet and fell over with Toast on top

54

of him. The dog buried his fangs into the wolf's neck.

"Toast has him!" John cried exultantly.

Father meantime had grabbed Toast by the back legs and was tugging to pull him off. Toast let go reluctantly and stood trembling with fury, his mouth dripping with blood and saliva.

David was stricken by a moment of terrible fear that the wolf would leap up and attack both his father and Toast. Instead, the wild beast remained on its back, its pointed snout uplifted, its belly exposed and vulnerable. Then it turned over with a whine, got to its feet, and with a frightening wail disappeared like a shadow into the forest.

Suddenly the scene was flooded with light as the jeep came around a turn of the road not thirty feet from where they were standing. Father and the boys were almost too dazed to realize that Ervin had actually arrived.

Ervin and his wife, Florence, came to a sudden stop at the unexpected scene illuminated by their headlights. There was Toast lying on the ground with Father, John, and David all appearing to be struggling over him. What they were doing was trying to get their arms around Toast to pull him to his feet and see if he was seriously injured.

Ervin and Florence climbed down from the jeep and hurried across the rough ground. They gave a hand in helping to bring Toast over to the jeep. Under the headlights, Father was able to make a thorough examination of the dog. Toast's long fur was so tangled and matted with blood that it was difficult at first to determine just where his wounds were. He bore up bravely under Father's poking and probing, only letting out a whine when a particularly painful spot was touched.

"Good Toast," Father said, soothing him. "Brave fellow. This isn't so bad." It appeared that the only serious damage consisted of two inch-long gashes along the middle of Toast's back. The wolf must have sunk his fangs there during the first go-round, when Toast evidently got the worst of it.

All at once Father laughed, partly in relief and partly because of Toast's expression of sadness and hurt dignity. Their noble protector and courageous warrior, the fierce beast of but a moment ago who had vanquished a timber wolf bigger than himself, permitted Father and Ervin to carry him like a child (a very large and heavy child, to be sure) and deposit him on a pile of blankets in the back seat of the jeep.

Only minutes later, they were all back at the camp. Father was delighted that Florence had come. Not only was she a wonderful cook, but as good a hand in the woods as any of them.

John rebuilt the fire and put the coffee pot on to heat. Everyone began to talk and the sound of their voices awakened Joe, who crawled out of his sleeping bag and came out by the camp fire to learn what had happened.

While John and David retold the story of the fight, Father cut away the fur around Toast's wounds and applied some antiseptic. Toast didn't care much for the taste of the stuff Father used, and went about cleansing the bites in his own way by licking them. Presently Father took Toast into the tent to bed down with Joe. It was the only way he could get Joe to go back in and to sleep.

The excitement subsided and the group around the camp fire sat quietly watching the flickering embers, the silhouettes of the trees, and the bleary moon fading behind the clouds over Lake Superior.

"The thing I can't understand," Father said, "is how we were able to pull Toast off that wolf. I thought for sure Toast was in for the kill."

"It sounds to me like the wolf surrendered," Ervin said."They aren't so fierce, you know. Never attack people unless cornered. Toast was out to protect you, so he carried the fight. But animals don't often fight to the death among their own kind—and wolves and dogs aren't so far apart in the family department. No, in a fight like that, when one of them is licked, he admits it and the other fellow usually lets him take off. People aren't always that sensible."

"No," Father said, "we aren't such sensible animals. Incidentally, we had a bad time with fog on the boat trip and if the skipper hadn't had such a brave crew, he would probably have panicked. As it was, we beat you here by hours. What happened to you?"

"We had compass trouble. Took a wrong fork of the road. Got all the way to Washburn before we knew it," Ervin said, spitting tobacco juice thoughtfully into the fire. Ervin chewed tobacco constantly and the boys regarded his skill in spitting, particularly from a moving vehicle, with amazed admiration.

"The trouble with the compass is that Ervin won't pay any attention to it," said Florence.

"I know," said Father. "I've traveled with Ervin."

"Think it's about time to pitch our tent and get some sleep, don't you, Florence?" said Ervin, spitting into the fire again with a sizzling splat.

v

Exploring Gold Hill

"Everybody up!" Father said, crawling out of his sleeping bag. Then he discovered to his surprise that he was really only talking to himself. Everybody *was* up!

The day was already bright. Father found Joe and Toast sitting outside the tent watching Florence prepare breakfast.

"Morning!" Florence called to him.

Father returned her greeting. He was more pleased than ever that she had come. Somehow it made the camp seem much jollier and almost homelike. "Where are the rest of the fellows?" he asked.

"They took the jeep down to the shore to haul in your boat," Florence said. She was a cheerful woman with a round face, blond hair, and large blue eyes, and she was known to be just as efficient as Ervin in north country

59

skills. In fact, when their neighbors couldn't find Ervin to give them a hand, they usually called upon Florence.

Father set off toward the shore, feeling a bit foolish about being the late riser. But yesterday *had* been a pretty full day, and he now felt wonderfully rested. He cast a backward glance over his shoulder and saw Toast bounding around the campsite with little Joe in lively pursuit. Evidently Toast's wounds from the night's encounter were giving him little or no trouble. Animals and children have wonderful recuperative powers, he thought. Given half a chance, they'll survive anything.

When he reached the shore, he found that Ervin and the boys had already beached the boat. He helped them secure the canvas over it to keep everything dry, regardless of the weather before their return. Then they all piled into the jeep and rode back to eat and break camp.

The sun was well up in a blue sky filled with racing white clouds by the time they had finished breakfast, packed their gear into the jeep, and climbed aboard. The wind was fresh with the clean smells of earth and water and filled with promise of a fine day. They were off—off into the Barrens and away to Gold Hill!

Except for the evergreens, the trees were still bare, but the tight little buds could be seen on their branches. The roads were slippery with moisture and cut with deep ruts, but Ervin drove skillfully and it didn't take long to cover the few miles from the channel to the base of Gold Hill.

Father sat up in the cab of the truck with Ervin and Florence, and the boys and Toast sat crowded together in the back amid the blankets and equipment. John wondered how things were with Mother and their sisters and small brothers back at the cottage. Everything was fine, he was sure.

"I wonder how those thieves made it without a jeep," John said, as the truck rocked and pitched over the rough course like a boat on choppy water.

"They may not have had to come quite as far," Ervin said. "In a hundred years, the shoreline can change. The level of the water keeps going down, so now the hill is a little farther inland."

Although they soon reached the base of the hill, it took a while to find a clearing that was suitable for a camp and accessible to the jeep. Ervin tried several trails branching from the main road before he found a spot that met with his approval. By the time they had set up their tents, it was almost noon. John and David collected dry branches and built a fire so Florence could fix a hot lunch for them. It turned out to be a spectacular production, consisting of everything from steak and potatoes to baked beans and hot dogs. Florence felt they had had a rather skimpy breakfast and she didn't want to let anyone set out exploring on an empty stomach.

After everyone was fed and the pots and pans had been washed in the creek that ran nearby, the group assembled at the jeep for instructions.

"I think we divide up," Ervin said. "The way to find something is to go slowly and look at everything. So we make teams and each team takes a small part of the land to go over carefully." Ervin spoke in a low voice that

61

carried just a trace of the accent of his Finnish fore-
bears. His manner was quiet, but when he spoke, everyone listened.

John spread his map on the ground and marked it at
the point where they were now gathered. "I'll orient the
map," he said, "and we can choose our territories." He

positioned the map so that its directions corresponded to the points on their compass. Everyone gathered around to see if they could pick out on the map the features of the country that they saw around them.

"I've figured this to be the route the thieves took," John said, pointing to the marks he had drawn. "So if I'm right, we don't need to go outside this general area." He inscribed a rough circle.

"Ya," said Ervin. "O.K., choose partners."

The teams consisted of Father and Joe, Florence and John, and Ervin and David.

"Synchronize your watches," Father said. "I want everyone back at camp by four o'clock. We'll need time to report on what we've seen and make plans for tomorrow. Of course," he added, "if you find the treasure, don't wait until four. Just bring it in!"

"One thing more," Ervin said. "Mark your routes as you go along. Break off branches or cut notches on the tree trunks. That way you won't get lost or cover the same ground twice without knowing it."

"Let's go," Father said. "Remember, back at four!"

Joe and Toast set off into the woods a few paces ahead of Father. They had only advanced a little way into the brush when Joe cried out in ringing tones, "I've found it! I've found it!"

All the others heard him and came running back, only to find Father shaking his head and saying, "False alarm," and little Joe tugging away at a partly buried, long abandoned wagon wheel.

"Not a bad find," Father told Joe, "but I think we'd better make this rule: no shouting unless you really need help. Otherwise we're going to confuse each other. Four o'clock is soon enough to tell what we've seen—or think we've seen. Come on now, let's all get going!"

Ervin and David started straight up the hill. David was extremely doubtful they would find anything in the way of hidden treasure, but he wondered what gleamed so brightly in the sun at the top of the hill. Besides, the fact that the hill was there seemed to David reason enough to climb it.

The slope was covered with pine and balsam as well as a great deal of birch. Since it was early spring, it was quite easy to make one's way up the hill in spite of its being so thickly grown with brush and timber. However, mud and crevices full of water occasionally made the footing difficult. Sometimes David's boot sank deep into the mud and he would have to pull his foot loose with a sucking noise.

"This isn't bad," Ervin told him. "It's *really* swampy down below in the hollows. You have to watch yourself there."

Near the top of the hill they found a birch tree that rose above the rest of the timber like an observation tower. Ervin gave David a boost up its thick trunk to a point where he could lock his arms and knees around it and, digging his heels into the bark, shinny up to where he could reach the branches and continue his climb until he was more than thirty feet above the ground.

David made himself comfortable astride a high branch and surveyed the scene. The beauty of the forested slopes, especially the tall cedars, sweeping heavenward like cathedral spires, made him catch his breath. Although he sometimes heard the sound of voices, he could not see any members of the party except Ervin, down below, scouting the area as though his life depended on it and blazing a trail by nicking a tree every twenty yards with a small, sharp hatchet.

It was a brilliant afternoon, but as far as David could see, there was not a glint of gold, just the dark green of the pines, the blue of the sky, and the long, shining expanse of Lake Superior. He shifted his position on his perch so that he could look northwest across the Barrens toward Bark Point. Something out there flashed and sparkled like a tub of silver. It was just a pond, of course, or a small inland lake, acting as a reflecting mirror to the particular angle of the sun. David laughed. This is like chasing the end of the rainbow, he thought.

Wherever you are, it always seems to be somewhere else. It occurred to him that if there was one place you could never see Gold Hill sparkle, it was probably on Gold Hill itself. Whatever caused the illusion, you had to be somewhere else to see it. "I'll have to tell Ervin," he said, and began carefully to work his way down the birch tree.

When David and Ervin arrived at the camp, they found Father and Joe at work getting the fire started. A moment later, John and Florence appeared. John had something cradled in his arms that moved and struggled against his chest. "Guess what," John called to them. "We found a fawn."

John set the fawn on the ground near Joe, who at once began to pet it gently. John and Florence had bound its feet to keep it from injuring itself while John carried it. John now untied it and the small creature wrestled itself to its feet, finding some difficulty in untangling its long, slender legs. It stood next to Joe, trembling, but letting him rub its nose and ears. It was a lovely animal and a mere baby, with the bare formation of a tail and its body beautifully marked with large brown spots. It stared at them with enormous brown eyes.

Father noticed that Toast was keeping his distance. He went over to Toast, who nuzzled his hands, then put his muddy feet up on Father's shoulders. Everyone laughed, and Father said, "The fawn is cute, all right, but let's have it understood that Mr. Toast is the most important."

66

"Maybe we'd better take the fawn back now, where we found him," Florence said. "His mother will be looking for him."

"Do you *have* to take him back?" Joe asked.

At this moment Toast shifted from his affectionate pawing of Father to an attitude of alertness. Father held Toast by the collar and pointed to the woods. "Look," he said, "and be very quiet."

Just beyond the clearing, a large, handsome doe stood in the gathering dusk, looking at them. In spite of the dog and the people, she stood her ground and whinnied ever so gently. The fawn bounded away from Joe and ran to its mother; then with scarcely a sound, the two of them disappeared.

"Gosh," said David, "did you ever see anything like that?"

"Just once before," Father said. "Remember, Ervin? David must have been younger than Joe then. You brought a fawn up to the cottage and we were standing right in the driveway by the car when its mother trotted up to get it, her tail going up and down like a trip hammer. You let the little fellow go and he went bounding after her. Remember?"

"Ya," said Ervin.

"This has been a great day, do you know it?" said David.

"It will be an even better one if everyone will lend a hand at getting supper," Father said.

Everyone had his share to do, and just a bit more, and everyone did it. Soon the camp was in shape, the supper served, and everyone was sitting around eating, laughing, and telling what he had seen during the afternoon's exploration. The ruins of an old logging camp had been found, creeks and ravines had been charted, the hill had been scaled and the general lay of the land noted, but no one had come upon a single clue to the secret they were searching for. Still, the smell of the night air was so fragrant, the wind from the lake so fresh, the fire so cheering and the sense of companionship so warm, that nobody felt in the least downhearted. Ervin's blue eyes sparkled and his weathered face glowed red in the fire-light above his broad shoulders and the scarf tied at the open neck of his woolen shirt. David, wrapped in his parka, with the hood folded flat against his shoulder blades, lay back and looked up at the stars while his father discussed their plans for tomorrow.

That seemed to be what Father was always talking about: tomorrow, what it could bring, what one should prepare for, what one should become. Tomorrow seemed to be the reason for everything.

David found himself dozing. Very faintly he heard the voices of the others:

"I'm turning in."

"Good night."

"So am I."

"Guess I will, too."

"Yep, me too. Tomorrow we've got to start looking in real earnest."

"That's for sure. Good night."

John dreamed that he had found the gold. But at the exciting moment of discovery, a shot rang out. The robbers were after him. He cried out in his sleep so loudly that David awoke and shook him.

"I'm being attacked," John explained.

"Go back to sleep," David told him. "I've saved you."

"Thanks," John said, and began to snore peacefully.

It was another bright morning when they all awoke. It was hard to believe their luck, for good weather did not often last long this time of year. David raced down to the stream with Joe and Toast to splash icy water in his face before helping with breakfast. John had already started the fire and Father was heating a pan of water for shaving. Florence surprised the boys by producing an accordion from the luggage and playing for them before breakfast while Ervin clapped and laughed. Soon she put the instrument down, however, and began preparing eggs and sausage and pancakes over the fire.

After the pans were washed and the camp tidied, they all gathered at the truck to review the day's plans. Ervin suggested that they concentrate on the base of the hill.

"Yesterday I had a really good time," he said. "Everybody did. David and I climbed the hill and looked at the view. Beautiful. Florence and John caught a fawn. Toast and Joe chased rabbits. Now today we look for gold.

"John and I studied that map and I think he has the right idea. Nobody with a heavy load could travel very far from the bottom of the hill. Now this hill is about seven miles around. If we break up into two groups and start out opposite ways, we can do a pretty carful job of looking before we meet halfway around at the other side."

Father, Joe, and David formed one team and Florence, Ervin, and John the other. Each group carried shovels, short axes, and a coil of strong rope. Even Joe wore a length of rope around his waist and a small pocketknife attached to his belt with a leather thong. Toast, of course, joined Joe's team. He always assumed responsibility for the smallest Brent present.

Since David had surveyed the entire area from the top of the hill, he took the lead of his party. It was interesting to try to relate the landmarks he had seen from a distance with the appearance of things at close hand. He tried to recall the changes of terrain he should expect—when the woods and brush would thin out and open into a clearing, which in turn would be bounded by rough gullies and rocky slopes before they entered the next extension of the forest.

He felt in high spirits. It was exhilarating to be in this wild and wonderful country just as spring was breaking forth. It was fun to be looking for something, even for something that might not really exist. The farther he walked and the more he looked, the less likely it seemed to him that any traces of a long-ago happening could remain here. There were no caves suggesting hidden mysteries to be explored, no intriguing crevices to tell them, "Dig here." There were just trees and brush and earth. Even the giant fallen trunks, victims of storm or age, were unlikely to mark the spot where hidden treasure lay. Besides, they were strewn everywhere. It would take an army to clear them out and search the ground beneath them.

70

It was fun to be looking. But David thought it would be more fun to know you were searching for something real, something you could be sure of. Everything in his life, it seemed to him, had been a game of play and pretend. What could the real thing be, he wondered, the real thing for David Brent? His family, of course, was very real and very much a part of him. But he was already a young man, and sooner or later he would be going away, somewhere, striving toward something.

David slogged on through the brush. In the beauty of the morning, everything in the world seemed possible. Even though he didn't know what it might be, he had the feeling that he was headed toward something. But what? Toward what landmark, what country, what glint, what shining mote over land or sea?

And I don't even have a compass! he thought.

All at once, David heard distant voices. He forgot his daydreams and hurried forward.

"Hey there!" John called to him, coming into view around the side of the hill. "Bet you didn't find what we did!"

vi

Where's Joe?

Father and Joe followed behind David at a considerable distance. Although they had no difficulty keeping up a good pace, they enjoyed stopping frequently to scout around or to rest on a fallen tree. At each such resting point, Joe took his knife and cut a mark on the log, which gave him a feeling of ownership.

Occasionally they spotted a small animal, a fox or rabbit or chipmunk, and Toast took off in delighted pursuit. Soon he would come crashing back through the brush. Father was having a wonderful time, too. Although he was keeping his eyes open for any interesting discoveries, he did not really have his mind on the idea of hidden wealth. The joy of being here was wealth enough; Joe's eager curiosity and the sight of David's tall form, seen through the bare branches striding far ahead of them with the practiced ease of an Indian guide, made him think of his own boyhood. Growing up in Chicago, he had played cowboys and Indians in city back yards and alleys. His greatest adventures were the ones he read about in books at the public library.

They skirted some low marshland which was already beginning to ooze and, rounding a sharp promontory of rock projecting from the hillside, suddenly heard John's voice and then caught sight of the rest of their party coming up a ravine and waving to them. Toast bounded ahead and soon overtook David, who had broken into a run to join the approaching trio.

Soon they were all together, exchanging greetings and finding dry places to put down their knapsacks and implements.

"What have you got to report?" David wanted to know.

"Wait a minute," John said, opening his knapsack and taking out one of the sandwiches Florence had prepared before they left camp.

"Come on, let's divide up the treasure," Father said. "I suppose you folks found it."

"Didn't *you*?" John said, grinning as though he knew something, but was going to take his time telling about it.

"Of course not," said David. "Tell us what you found."

Father noticed that Ervin was also smiling mysteriously. "What's up?" he said.

"Nothing, maybe," Ervin said. "But what do you think of this?" He reached into his parka and extracted

73

a flat piece of wood about a foot long. One edge of it was bound with deeply corroded metal and the other had a circular cutout in it.

"Well, I'm glad someone found *something*," Father said. "What is it?"

"We think it came from an old chest," John said, excitedly. "What else would have brass reinforcements and a cutout place for a lock? Erv says it's walnut."

"It's not a very big piece," Ervin said, "but you can see by the tongue and grooving, it's good workmanship."

"How in the world did you spot it?" Father asked. It occurred to him that even though the leaves and grass were not yet out, there could have been a full-sized trunk lying in the brush and he probably wouldn't have seen it.

"Anything that's regular, perfectly straight," Ervin said, "you know that isn't nature—that's man-made."

"Where do we start digging?" said David.

Ervin shook his head. "I don't know," he said. "We looked around, but there's no way to tell. Maybe it washed down from somewhere. Maybe someone broke it up and scattered the pieces. No way to tell. But it sure enough looks to me like it came from an old chest."

"Where'd you find it?" Father said.

"Down there, just before we came in sight of you," John said, pointing.

Toast, with the instant reflexes of a trained hunting dog, went streaking off in the direction John had indicated.

75

"Let Toast find it," Father said. "I'm ready for my sandwiches."

"If we think about this, we may find the answer," Ervin said. "When I am making something and I don't know just how to go about it, then I must stop and think. But you have to take your time. If you hurry up and try something, you go wrong. You must think it through.

"Now we believe it was about this time of year these gold robbers came here. It was an early spring, maybe, like now. So if the gold was in a chest, they couldn't pull it over the ice. And like John says, they couldn't carry it very far, either. Suppose it was raining and they were really stuck. What would they do?"

"They could have buried it," John said. "That was my theory."

"Ya," Ervin said. "That's what everybody thinks. But the Army was chasing them. Did they have time? Did they have spades? Did they want to wait a long time before they came back for their money? Maybe they just smashed up the box and divided the money."

"And ran off every man for himself," David said.

"It's possible," Father said.

"But the money never turned up," John said.

"Ya, nor maybe the men, either," said Ervin, gazing across the Barrens. "If they didn't know the country, I doubt they got out."

There was silence as they munched their sandwiches.

"Where's Joe?" Florence asked.

"Huh?" said David. "Hey, Toast! Get Joe!"

"Where's Toast?" said Father.

76

"He went chasing off when I pointed," John said. "Maybe Joe went after him."

They all started out at a run in the direction Toast had taken.

vii

In the Bog

Following John's lead, they scrambled down the hillside, tripping and sliding and grabbing hold of one another for support. In spite of their haste, John rapidly outdistanced the rest and disappeared into the brush.

It flashed through Father's mind that they really did not know where they were heading, but once started down a hill it was difficult to come to a stop.

"Hold up!" he shouted. His feet skidded out from under him and before he could recover his balance, David tumbled on top of him. Ervin and Florence, who were close behind, tried to stop, slipped, and pitched forward onto the heap.

For a moment, Father thought that all of Gold Hill had fallen on him. Then as the bodies on top of him began to untangle themselves, he found he could move and, with an effort, sit up.

78

"Are you hurt?" David asked.

"No," Father said. He wasn't quite sure, but he knew they had something more important to do than pile on top of each other like football players. "Is everybody all right?" he asked.

"Ya," said Ervin. "Let's try again. Better let Florence and me show you how."

"The slow way is best," Father said, getting to his feet. "Anyway, probably nothing has happened to Joe. He couldn't have gone far and he'll be safe with Toast."

"Down here, you don't have to go far to get lost," Ervin said.

As they made their way down the slope, the reason for Ervin's concern became clear. From the forested heights of the hill, the low land looked open and easy to travel. As they got down to it, however, they found this flat country overgrown with brush and clumps of high reeds.

"There's John!" David said.

Some distance ahead, they saw John making his way back to them and shaking his head. They waited for him to join them.

"No sign of Joe or Toast," he said. "It's muddy down here, too. Watch your step."

"Let's fan out and start calling for them," Father said. "But keep in sight of each other."

Their voices carried across the brush-covered flat land and the boggy hollows and echoed from the side of the hill.

"Joe! Toast!"

There was no answer. It was a clear, fine day, but David felt a twinge of fear like that which had seized him when the fog closed in around their boat out in the lake. He sensed hidden danger.

John marched ahead, calling for Joe and Toast. He was worried by their disappearance, but it did not strike him as logical that anyone could get lost so quickly. If it wasn't logical, then it wasn't likely. Therefore it shouldn't be long before they ran across the missing boy and dog.

Father and Ervin scouted along the edges of a small marsh. "Do you think they could have gone in there?" Father asked, looking at the tall reeds and the dangerously soggy ground. Ervin said nothing, but he and Father exchanged alarmed glances.

David pressed on, using his arms like a swimmer to spread the reeds and scratchy brush aside and stumbling from time to time when his toe caught in the dried marsh grass or his feet slipped on sudden patches of ooze. He had a terrible thought: "What if we don't find them?" Once the idea lodged in his mind, he had to admit to himself that this was possible. The worst *could* happen. Joe and Toast might disappear in the bog and never be found.

The bright sunlight no longer seemed joyful. Instead, it seemed cruel. But David knew there was nothing to do but keep on going. . .keep on looking.

Meanwhile, Florence made her way toward some higher ground in hope of getting a better view. As she stood scanning the flat lands and listening to the shouts of the other members of the party, it seemed to her that she detected another sound.

It was more like a whine than a bark, but she was

sure it was an animal sound and not too distant. She shared Ervin's keenness of sight and his knowledge of the country, but the ground cover was so thick that it took her several minutes to distinguish a splotch of red which she was certain must be Toast's fur. She gave a cry and started out, leaping across a gully and speeding down a slope that led to a hollow concealed by reeds and bushes. She ran toward it, agile as a deer, her brown ski pants and plaid mackinaw flashing over the rough, dun-colored ground.

As she parted the brush, she saw Toast sitting in the mud with shoulders hunched and feet widely spread. He was whining piteously.

"Toast!" she called. "Where's Joe?"

"Here!" cried a small voice.

To her astonishment, she saw Joe's head peeping from behind Toast's haunches. She rushed forward and, grasping Toast's forelegs, began tugging with all the strength that was in her. The dog struggled to his feet and behind him came Joe, floundering in mud up to his waist and hanging on for dear life to Toast's tail!

Florence went down on her knees and, locking her arms around him, pulled Joe the rest of the way out of the mud pit into which he had been sucked.

The moment they were clear of the mire, Toast threw back his head and uttered a resounding call that quickly summoned the others. David was the first to reach them.

"Don't come too close. You'll sink!" Florence warned him, still hugging Joe in her arms.

David paid no attention. He flung himself upon Joe and lifted him up onto his shoulders. Toast bounded for-

81

ward with a yelp of delight and began pawing them furiously, his tail waving bravely and throwing mud in all directions.

In a moment everyone was there, each trying joyfully to get his arms around everyone else. No one cared if he got smeared with mud from head to foot, and the sun shone down on them now with a warm and cheerful light.

Ervin's first thought was that they should take Joe back to Bark Point immediately. But as Ervin had learned, it was easy enough to get lost in the Barrens by daylight without chancing it at night. Since it was getting late in the day, they returned to camp instead, got Joe out of his damp and muddy garments, and tucked him into his sleeping bag.

"Nothing's wrong with me. Let me up," Joe complained. But his teeth were chattering and Florence insisted that he have his supper "in bed."

"This wrecks things for sure," John told David when they were banking the fire for the night. "I knew something would happen if we brought Joe."

"Do you feel so bad about it?" David asked.

"No, I guess I really don't," John said. "I'm glad Joe's O.K. But I wish we could have spent more time digging around where we made our find. In spite of what Ervin says, they could have left more behind than a broken-up chest. There could be some treasure somewhere."

"It wasn't Joe's fault he got stuck," David said. "He's

been a good scout all along. We always told him to stick close to Toast."

"It wasn't Toast's fault, either," John said. "But just once, I'd like to see something come off just the way we planned it."

"You'll wait a long time for that," David told him. "Anyway, it's been quite an adventure."

"Nothing really happened except for Joe getting caught in the mud," John said. "I was scared, but I don't think he would have sunk all the way. Not very soon, anyhow."

"I wouldn't bet," David said. "I sort of feel as if I've been through everything in the world."

"Another few days and it will be back to the old routine for all of us," John said.

"I'm ready," David said. "I'm sure now I can face anything."

The next morning, after a quick breakfast, they all drove to the shore, where Ervin helped Father and David and John launch the boat. Although Joe was none the worse for his experience, Florence insisted that she and Ervin would take him to Bark Point in the jeep. Toast would of course accompany them.

Joe stood on the pier with Ervin and Florence and Toast and waved to Father and the boys until the boat had passed through the channel and was far out on the lake. Then they climbed into the jeep and drove off over the bumpy roads through the wilderness. Joe found the trip very exciting. Ervin minded his compass and took all the proper turns to bring them to their destination.

"Do you think we'll beat the boat this time?" Florence asked.

"Ya," said Ervin, chewing placidly on his tobacco, "if we can't get there before the boat, I think I'll quit driving."

viii

Joe's Secret

Back at the Point, no one was quite sure when to expect the return of the Gold Hill expedition. But the days were so pleasant that Mother had scarcely any worries about how the adventurers were faring.

No one was at a loss for things to do. Susan had been across the field talking with Bill Roman. He told her about what he was sure must have been dinosaur tracks which he had once come upon in the rocks near one of the tiny inland lakes where he fished. She made him promise to take her there to look for them when the family came back for the summer.

On her way home, she stopped on the beach to see if she could find any new stones. One of her summer projects was going to be to classify all of the rocks in her collection. She had always loved pretty stones and kept those that seemed particularly attractive or interesting. Recently she had been reading about geology, about how the very substance of the earth had come into being and how its history is recorded in rock formations. She had very definitely decided to become a geologist.

She came into the cottage with a handful of stones. Mother was making lunch in the kitchen. Joshua was sleeping. Amy and Lisa were playing with Adam on the porch. Everything was very peaceful. It gave Susan a feeling of deep, quiet happiness just to sit down by the window in the warm sun and look at her new rocks. One of them sparkled with golden metallic specks. Fool's gold, it was called, because it looked like gold but actually was formed from iron or copper.

Susan felt a twinge of loneliness for Joe and her older brothers. It struck her they had been decidedly unfair not to take her along with them. A girl geologist could easily have been of great help.

Just then she heard the sound of a car coming up the drive. Running to the porch, she saw the jeep pull up with Joe sitting in the front seat between Ervin and Florence. Before anyone else could get out, Toast leaped from the back seat and came bounding up the porch steps to greet her.

"Mother!" Susan shouted. "They're here! Part of them, anyway."

Mother came running from the kitchen and nearly fell over Toast.

"Goodness," she said. "I didn't expect anyone back so soon."

In a moment, Joe came flying up the steps and threw

himself into his mother's arms. Ervin and Florence were close behind, and since everyone was intent upon telling his story, it was several minutes before things became calm enough for any one person to be heard. Finally Amy and Lisa stopped jumping up and down and Mother released Joe from her embrace and Susan quit shouting questions and Toast settled down. It looked as though at any moment order might be restored.

"Please come in and sit down," Mother said to Ervin and Florence. "I have lunch just about ready and if you'll all give me ten seconds, we can eat and you can tell us everything that's happened."

"Well, first of all," Florence said, as soon as they were seated at the table, "we brought you quite a laundry problem."

"You should see my parka!" Joe said. "It's all mud!"

"You should have seen Joe," Ervin said. "All mud, too! We took quite a lot of it off, but there is still work to be done, unless I'm mistaken."

Mother took a closer look at Joe, and sure enough, his hair was caked with mud and so were his trousers and boots. "What on earth happened?" she asked.

"It was like this," Ervin said. "We were all out hunting gold and about noon we joined up for lunch and we started talking. We got so wrapped up in all the ideas we were telling that we paid no attention until all of a sudden, Florence said, 'Where's Joe?' We all looked around, and nobody knew. We didn't know where he was or how long he'd been gone."

"I was with Toast," Joe said.

"We started searching," Florence said, "and finally,

89

down in a hollow, I spotted Toast. I yelled at him, but he wouldn't move. He was just sitting there. No sign of Joe."

"I was underneath," Joe said.

"Under *Toast?*" Mother said.

"He was for sure," said Ervin. "He was just about under the ground, that's where he was. Up to his arms in quick mud."

"Quick *mud?*" Mother said.

"Ya," said Ervin. "Like quicksand, only mud. You slip into it and you can't get out. It sucks you in."

Mother turned pale. "Oh, Joe!" she said.

"I was all right," Joe said. "I hung onto Toast."

"That's why the dog wouldn't move when I called," Florence said. "Joe had him by the tail!"

"Gracious," Mother said. "Poor Joe. And poor Toast. He hates having his tail pulled. It hurts him terribly."

"As long as Joe could hold out, so could Toast," Florence said. "He was braced there forever, if need be. Nothing in the world could have moved him till we got Joe out of the mud."

"Wonderful Toast," Mother said, patting him. Then she studied Joe. "We've just got to get the sauna bath going," she said. "It's the only thing that will ever clean that boy up!"

"I'll start the stove heating for you," Ervin said.

He went outside to the bathhouse that one of the Brents' Finnish neighbors had constructed for them. It was a small shed with clean-smelling cedar walls and a wood stove in the corner. Rocks from the beach were

90

piled on top of the stove. Ervin started a brisk fire in the stove. As soon as the stones were hot, he called Joe, who came running out robed in a large bath towel.

Joe threw a pail of water over the stones, and the steam rose with a great hiss, filling the shed. There were three wooden steps in front of the stove. Joe sat on the first one, shutting his eyes and letting the hot steam envelop him. Then he moved up to the next step, where it was hotter still. Beside the steps was a bucket of water and a small switch of maple leaves called a "vichta." From time to time, Joe took the switch and splashed his chest and shoulders with its wet leaves. It felt wonderful.

A true Finn would complete his bath by running from the shed, pink as a lobster, and jumping into the cold lake. Since there was still ice on the lake, Mother told Joe to leave out this step. So instead he poured some water over his head, wrapped the towel around him, and went back to the house feeling like a new boy.

Mother found fresh clothes for him to put on. Then she collected his camping garments and started to take them into the laundry room.

Ervin, who had been unloading things from the jeep, came in bearing Joe's muddy parka. Mother gazed at it hopelessly.

"Well, just throw it on top of the pile," she said. "We'll see what can be done for it."

"Empty the pockets," Joe said. "I found some big pennies."

"I'm afraid they'll be muddy, too," Mother said, but

she put her hands into the mud-caked pockets anyway.

"Pennies!" she said, fingering several coins about the size of half dollars. "Where did you get these?"

"In the mud," Joe said. "Before I sank."

Ervin took one of the coins, holding it up to the

light and wiping the grime off with his thumb. "Ya," he said. "A twenty-dollar gold piece."

"He has three of them!" Mother said, taking them over to the sink to clean them. "Where did they ever come from?"

"That stolen money," Ervin said. "It might not have been buried. Maybe it just sank. Maybe the robbers, too, were all swallowed up."

"Do you think these really might be part of the robbers' loot?" Mother said, holding up a shimmering golden coin she had scoured. It had a liberty head on one side and an American eagle on the other, but the inscription was too worn to read.

"Can we go back and find the rest?" Susan asked excitedly. "It's the robbers' gold. I know it!"

As it turned out, she was almost certainly right. David later took the gold pieces to a coin expert and learned that the coins were over one hundred years old and exactly what one would expect to find in the shipment described in Wilbur Brookshaw's story. For the present, however, they could only make a pretty good guess that Joe had found what they were looking for.

"That low land is a bad place," Ervin told Susan. "I don't think you'll find anything else there except a good place to sink. Maybe these are all the coins that are left. Maybe not. Probably it all washed down into the bottom of the marsh, years and years ago. It's all gone, except for a piece or two you might find by luck. That Joe is a lucky fellow."

"Can I have my pennies back?" Joe asked.

"Joe, you found the treasure!" Mother said.

"Oh," said Joe. "Are they the treasure? I thought we were looking for a big box."

They heard the distant sound of a motor and looking out at the bay saw the boat coming in.

Father and the boys waved toward the cottage. Father was glad the return trip had gone so easily, and he was relieved to see Ervin's jeep parked in the driveway. And there were still a few days left to get in some trout fishing, he thought happily.

John was thinking that it would be awfully good to be back again with his entire large family. It really wasn't so bad to have so many brothers and sisters. In fact, it wasn't bad in the least.

David climbed out on the prow, making ready to tie up when they reached the dock. It had been a very unusual trip, he thought. Somehow, he had learned things that he could not quite express, but which seemed to make a difference. There was more to Gold Hill than met the eye.

As the boat came alongside the dock, Mother and Ervin and Florence looked at each other awkwardly, wondering how they were going to break the news to Father and the boys that little Joe had brought the secret of Gold Hill back in his pocket.

Toast jumped to his feet and began pawing at the porch door.

"Let him out, Susan," Mother said. "He can go down to the dock and tell them. After all, he and Joe were in on the find together."

"Toast can't talk," Amy said severely.

"Mother's joking," Susan said.

"No, I'm not," said Mother.

94

INDEX

My work in progress:

Word On Another
Country

Exercises in family biography are among the most innocent and instructive of literary endeavors and should be encouraged on the part of our progeny. Only in the memory of others does our existence acquire substance and clarity. In our own minds, our lives remain a confused muddle, useful at times for creative fabrication, but in the end lacking objective reality as well as rhyme or reason. It is through the eyes of others that we have actually existed, been seen, and acquired distinct properties as objects and forces. Thus it is entirely true that being is spiritual rather than material, for the records of our existence is carried in the psychic fabric of those who encounter us. Only their memory can trap our being as objective fact (which to us dissolves in a perpetual series of transformation). Conversely, our memories of others and the stories of our for-bearers seem, quite properly, to take place in another country, a separate reality that exists somewhere outside the world of flux in which we daily participate.

The subjective really provides nothing to write about, although it provides everything we need to bring to the perceptive and descriptive grasp of lives other than our own, including the imaginary. Good art can be created through an imaginary "I", but the moment the artist means it when he says, "I", he is lost.

...to be continued.

To Have a Father

By

Stuart Brent

CHICAGO TRIBUNE MAGAZINE

When I was a child I often dreamed of my brother who was a cowboy in Texas and of a half-understood world of glory and disaster summoned up by stories that my parents told. One such tale marked both an end and a beginning in the lives of the immigrant family from Kiev of whom I was the last born, a product of my mother's forty-third year.

This story sparkled with visual appeal: snow swirling in bright streaks about the lighted facade of a neighborhood theater. It quickened the heart with blatant wish-fulfillment, then, like all infantile dreams, took a strange turn that corrupted its sweetness.

On a January night in 1913, two thirteen-year old boys huddled near the marquee of the Jewish Palace Theater on the west side of Chicago. The other members of their gang had either made it inside the theater or slipped away. My brother, Dave, and his fellow delinquent stamped their feet and kept watch for failure of alertness on the part of the man in the box office. They were very cold.

The boys were about to give up their vigil when a flutter of paper clips, which proved to be green certificates, began descending upon them. They set about collecting them in the hope they might prove to be United Cigar Store coupons, a valued form of tender discarded only by smokers of great wealth or insane profligacy. The green blizzard continued but briefly. After they had caught what they could and thoroughly scrounged the area for the rest, Dave and his friend retired to a faintly lighted entry hall to count their coupons. There, in a moment of ecstasy and terror, they discovered the slips were twenty dollar bills, apparently real ones.

The boys stuffed the currency into their coat pockets and decided to seek adult counsel.

My father, Joseph Brodsky, was then thirty-four years old, a lean, handsome man with a black moustache and a fair knowledge of America and its ways, for he had come to this country from the Ukraine in 1901, a year after Dave was born.

Dave feared his father, and not without reason, for he was a poor student and frequently found himself in trouble. But there was no question about taking a matter of this magnitude to any but the highest mortal source of judgement. Taking his companion and their booty to his father was perhaps the first and last decisive action of poor Dave's life.

They counted the money on the kitchen table. It amounted to $11,000!

7

Father said, "In Europe, anyone who finds something is entitled to half of it. But not in this country. I will advertise in the newspaper and we'll wait and see what happens."

The money was hidden beneath a floor board and for six weeks they waited. No one responded to the advertisement. Father and David then paid a momentous call on the other boy's father and presented him with $5,500.

To Joseph Brodsky, the fortune scattered from above the theater was a heavenly sign to which he could respond only in one way: by reestablishing for himself and his family the roots they had left when they fled the pogroms of their homeland. He had been a farmer and blacksmith in the old country. To own, at last, in this country, with freedom and dignity, a piece of farmland far from the city was to realize his true destiny.

At the nearby real estate firm of Greenwald and Norris, he consulted with Mr. Bernard Greenwald, who sold him eighty acres of land near Foley, Alabama, sixty acres of which were purported to be cleared for farming and graced with a house and a well.

Father and David said farewell to my mother and to the children: Harry, David's elder brother, and Anne, Mary, and Rose. They departed by train with a huge trunk, largely filled with tools, and with a supply of tremendous sandwiches and a container of tea adequate for the three-day journey through the plains of Illinois, the hills of Tennessee, and the pine wilderness of the deep South.

Foley lies south of Mobile, within twenty-five miles of the Gulf of Mexico. Upon their arrival, Father and Dave went to the sherrif's office, where they found a kindly man who addressed them with a German accent. Since Father could speak German, a warm relationship sprang up between the two men.

The first things my father needed, the sheriff told him, were a horse and wagon. Yes, he knew exactly where both might be purchased. The price was $80, and since the mare was in foal, my father thought this a bargain.

Guided by the sheriff, they followed a dirt country road eight miles to the farm. There Pa discovered that instead of sixty acres being cleared, as represented, only ten were suitable for farming. Nevertheless, he set about putting in a crop of peas, for which the sheriff assured him there was a ready market in Pensacola, Florida, thirty miles distant. He also went to work on the house, adding to one side of it and building a screened-in bedroom for David.

He cut down a large tree and scooped out the inside of trunk so it could be filled with water as a horse trough. He bought chickens and planted peas, corn, and lettuce. Once he thought he had located a supply of wild lettuce, which he made into a sumptuos salad, only to discover after the first bite that it was tobacco!

Aided by Dave and the horse, Pa worked from morning to night, then relaxed by reading, in the light of a kerosene lamp, one of the three books he brought with him: one contained the essays of Charles Lamb and Robert Louis Stevenson, another consisted of lectures on evolution by Charles Darwin, and the third was a Yiddish book of fairy tales.

Almost from the first, my father recognized the hopelessness of it. Surrounded by forest and underbrush which it would take years to clear, it was impossible to put in crops adequate to sustain a family. The horse was high strung, did not care greatly for work, and frequently ran back to her original owner. Then David would have to hike the ten miles to where that farmer lived and ride the truant horse bareback.

David did not relate well to the mare or her colt, but he adored a calf they had acquired. After nine months, when Father knew that the farm project was a failure, the most painful part for David was selling the calf.

When the letter arrived telling Mother that Pa was giving up and coming back to Chicago, she cried, softly and helplessly, for three days. She, too, loved farming and had shared my father's dreams. Now what would become of them?

The dreamer came back to look for a job. He was stern with himself. "A man must suffer," he said.

Dave, who had been a poor student before, now dropped out of school and at the age of fourteen persuaded a recruitment officer that he was sixteen and enlisted in the army. He served as a bugler in World War I and, after being mustered out, gravitated to Texas, where he worked on a cattle ranch.

I was born during the war, but it was years later that Dave again returned home and I met my "true" brother, whose heroic existence I had shared in my dreams. I regarded him as my "true" brother both because of my identification with his exciting life and because my other brother, Harry, was so much older, lived apart from us with his own family

9

(including a son whom I detested), and he simply did not seem like a brother. How wonderful it must be, I thought, to have a brother to play with. All I had were sisters and they were no fun at all.

My sisters assured me that Dave had been a boy of infectious charm and outstanding good looks, with jet black hair and great black eyes. What none of us knew, of course, was that Dave had turned mean.

The day my father received a letter announcing Dave's decision to come home for a visit was an occasion of intense excitement. My mother started at once to prepare the house for him. Our flat had numerous huge rooms, only two of which were bedrooms: one off the dining room which was occupied by my three sisters, and one off the kitchen, where my mother and father slept. I slept on a day bed that was unfolded nightly in the dining room.

The great room, however, was the parlor, which was never occupied except by the most important visitors or used for state occasions, such as the death of an aunt. It could be looked at, but woe to me if my mother caught me stepping across the invisible barrier which separated it from our normal living quarters. The sight alone, however, was an aesthetic experience of some magnitude. The furniture was all bought at the store on 12th Street called Hartman's. On the day it was acquired, we all went to this great store and my mother and my sisters chose each piece after much study and deliberation.

I can still see this special furniture being uncrated in our flat, with my mother anxiously in attendance to make certain each object was in perfect condition, her "jewels" from the shana store.

The rug which covered the floor was russet with a gold border, floating softly on the shining surface of varnished hardwood. A large bay window faced directly over Douglas Park, about whose trees that radiant light which we see only in childhood slanted through the Venetian blinds (they were the latest thing) and patterned the pale, white walls with bright horizontal shafts and glowed on the dark, polished furnishings, the mahogany sofa with it velvet upholstery and the outrageously coiffured curls which bedecked the legs of the center table.

Our flat was on the third floor of a building which housed virtually every living member of my family, uncles and aunts, cousins and near cousins. By this time, my father had become assistant to the master tool and die maker at the AmercianCar and Foundry Company. He was unhappy with tenement life and was saving his money to buy a house. The building was presided over by a small, dark landlord with gnarled hands and the sharp face of a petulant imp. His response to every request for service was, "Movcha! Movcha!" It seemed impossible to me that this miserable gnome, with his compulsive scream of "Move! Move!" could belong to the same species as a man like my father, who had the power to crush him like a roach and the dignity to ignore him entirely.

My father had two sisters, each as strong and as tall as he. My father's eldest sister, Leah, was a brilliant and gifted lady. Her drawing was masterful. She married a man as sweet and gentle, if by no means as large and talented, as herself. The other sister, Ida, was not nearly as pretty or intelligent, but she was the favorite of my grandmother, who was greatly concerned about getting a suitable husband for her. She therefore selected and landed for her daughter a man of unusual qualities, learned in the Torah and its interpretation. When he and his bride came to America, he naturally assumed the role of a gentleman, for he did not believe in work. Study was his metier, and it was the duty of others to support him. Thus they lived in our large tenement building without visible source of income. I have no idea how they managed.

The morning David arrived, he appeared just as I had imagined, a hero of godlike beauty and the very figure of an ideal brother. My father fell upon his neck and kissed him and wept. All of us and our vast swarm of relatives were swept away in the joy of the prodigal's return! I then withdrew from the scene with fever a swollen jaw and spent the next several weeks recovering from the mumps.

I was a good patient and was rewarded by the present of a complete new outfit of clothes, given to me a piece at a time during my confinement. On the Sabbath when I was judged well, my mother helped me get dressed in these loved garments in the bedroom off the dining room, while the rest of the family stood outside the door, waiting for me to emerge.

First, there was new pair of the long, fleece-lined underwear which I wore ten months out of the year, then my new stockings, new shirt, new suit, and new shoes. Now it was all complete, and my mother held open the door. I came forward with my heart bursting for approval, a small boy attired in brown corduroy jacket and knickers, yellow cotton-wool stockings, and a pair of yellow work shoes. My shorts had brown checks and yellow stripes. As I entered the dining room, I saw my father standing apart from the others and my spirits leaped, but my vision blurred. Only the furnishings remained in focus, the Tiffany lamp hanging low over the round oak table and damask tablecloth, the straight-backed chairs, and centered against the wall between two large windows, the severe black sofa. The windows were draped with other curtains held back with tasseled brown ties, and opposite stood the oak highboy in whose large drawers my mother stored the sheets and pillowcases and towels, and beneath which my cat, Buddha, periodically had her kittens. The highboy was surmounted with a beveled mirror before which my sisters combed their hair while awaiting use of the bathroom and which I employed for philosophical purposes, making faces and wondering what would become of me. Would I be President? No, better to be like my father. Father was everything.

Now I came forward to shouts of laughter. I caught my father's smiling look. My mother turned to my sisters and whispered something. On display and sensing my importance, I began to grin and grimace. The brilliance of my yellow shoes overwhelmed me and I silently vowed never to scuff them, but to polish them each day and guard them from all harm. My heart overflowed with goodness and joy.

"Pa," said my brother, Dave, in a harsh voice. "Now all you have to do is give him a pushcart and he can start selling bananas."

In the bitter silence that followed, my face contorted and I began to sob. The world darkened around me and I forgot my new suit, my adoring father and my mother and sisters, and crumpled before the brother who had cut me so terribly.

When my father became angry, everyone had a way of disappearing. He telegraphed the anger simply by a look from those deep brown eyes, which when they were not gentle, could flame in the most terrifying way. It was all over in a moment, and I was quickly consoled as my father placed his hand softly on my drooping eight-year-old shoulders and announced, "Tomorrow we go to the Municipal Pier for a boat ride. No one can come along. Just the two of us."

There was a rustle of sisters in motion and a rebuke from my mother to the abashed David, "How can you say things like that to a child? How can you?" Then she led me back to the bedroom to change into another outfit until tomorrow, when I would wear my new attire for the promised boat ride.

Going on the boat would just be part of it. The excursion also meant

12

a tremendous streetcar ride, the spectacle of countless people, and unlimited indulgence in popcorn, ices, peanuts, taffy apples, and, above all, cotton candy! The vertigo of anticipation was nearly as great as that which was certain to ensue from performance.

On the bright early Sunday morning, my father and I left the flat to wait for the streetcar on the corner of California Avenue and 12th Street. It was but a block to the corner, yet at least a dozen compatriots greeted my father on the way. "Hello, Joe." "Good morning, Joe." "Where are you off to with you _mizenka_ (your youngest and last)?" Some spoke perfect English, some Yiddush, others a kind of pidgin English. But all were Jews. The feeling of yiddish was in the air; you could sense it in the buildings, on the sidewalk, and in the park across the street, where old men sat on benches, talking and flailing the air with their arms.

Just before we reached the corner, my mother's sole relative in America approached. He was on his way to pay our family a visit. My father disapproved of him for various reasons, including the fact that he was living with a woman, while his wife remained in Russia. Hence, my father addressed him only as "kozick" (cousin), never by name.

"And where are going?" Kozick asked indulgently. He had quite a successful business as a customer-peddler selling merchandise on a time payment plan to Poles and Lithuanians. His dress was modest except for the pearl gray spats and blazing tie which were his stylistic trademark. Although a rather tall man, his face was round and his eyes very, very small, while his chin disappeared into the comfortable layer of fat around his neck.

Responding in his most precise night school English, my father said, "I am taking my pride and joy for a boat ride and to see the sights of Municipal Pier." Then he looked down at me and beamed.

Kozick nodded his head vigorously, as if to say, "You have my entire permission." Withdrawing his hand from his pocket, he offered me a penny, saying with a smile, "Buy something nice from me."

I hesitated to accept until a touch at my elbow by my father signaled permission to extend my hand. The civilities of our meeting were completed with an exchange of goodbyes, and at last we were on our way and standing at the trolley stop. My whole being vibrated. I wanted to leap and dance. Sometimes one waited forever for the streetcar, but today I didn't mind. I would dance and vibrate until it came. And come it did,

13

almost immediately, bearing down upon us at prodigious speed, a pitching red dragon which came to a grinding halt before us as the motorman sprayed the wheels with sand and applied the brakes.

The car was already crowded, with the brown woven cane-covered seats fully occupied and numerous passengers gripping the straps that depended from rods above the aisle. But it was still possible to get in. The situation did not yet require boarding passengers to cling to metal handgrips outside the car above the steps as part of a swarming human overflow that billowed perilously as the car sped swaying down the street.

Riding the streetcar was a contact sport, for no one from our neighborhood traveled without his arms full of something — fruit or sausage or schmaltz herring wrapped loosely in a newspaper, bundles of old clothing or dirty laundry or just plain junk, baggage of all sorts — and there was no place to stow anything. Conflict was inevitable, but it took the form largely of outrageous threats which were greeted with general hilarity by the spectators.

"I'll tear out your gorgul!"

"I'll take your kishkes and twist them into a knot and stuff your balls with them!"

"May you grow a pimple on the end of your nose!"

It was frightening and delicious.

Our trolley served the tenement districts then occupied by Jews who had immigrated from Russian and Middle Eastern territories where the foot of an oppressor was ever on their necks. To learn to accept their new freedom, master a new language, adopt new customs, gain the ability to earn a living, even to look someone straight in the eye, called for a tremendous psychic reorientation. Only time and the safety of a familiar habitat could allay such mistrust and fear. I was raised on the warning, "Der Yid mis man schmissen." The Jew is always whipped! Say nothing. Keep to yourself. Fear of the goyim entered into every moment of a child's early training. It fortified the boundaries between ethnic neighborhoods, beyond which, although there might be peace and business intercourse, one trespassed with certain knowledge that one was among enemies.

The streetcar was a transitional device which permitted a commingling on neutral, if unsteady, ground, of old and new, familiar and exotic. Rabbis with long beards and black, round hats sat silently or conversed in whispers as though unaware of the pressing crowd which lurched forward at each screeching stop. A catastrophe seemed barely avoided at every corner. My father and I stood at the rear of the car, commanding a strategic view of the street scene retreating behind us. The conductor stood nearby on the platform between two open doors which served respectively for entrance to the seating area to exit therefrom. Like an experienced sailor, he remained imperturbably upright without regard for vagaries of momentum or the ever-changing inclination of the deck.

A change of streetcars finally brought us to Grand Avenue and the lake. Grand Avenue did not even in those days match the dignity of its name, but its terminus at the foot of Lake Michigan defied belief. The Chicago Municipal Pier, extending into the lake form the streetcar turnaround, presented every mode of architectural magnificence: domes and towers, tiered galleries, flagpoles and banner. It was immense. Its halls and corridors, balconies and decks followed endlessly. And every foot of it seemed devoted to perpetual carnival. The profusion of food offerings, amusement devices, music, human bodies and inhuman cacophony swept me into a state of exhilaration both alarming and blissful.

Our destination was the very end of the pier where excursion boats docked to take on passengers. There the lake breeze calmed me and the splash of waves muted the din of revelry. We stood at the water's edge by a protective bundle of pilings, watching a boat approach.

The wake of the boat broke against the wall of the pier and to my horror a monster rose out of the water --- a bloated corpse, huge, black, grotesque.

There were cries from nearby spectators, but I had lost my capacity to speak. I felt my father's strong arm about me, pulling me away from the specter and the screaming crowd.

Inside the rotunda of the pier, my father led me to the ice cream stand. I was now sobbing hysterically, but as he handed me the cone and I looked into his face, I perceived an expression of such unconditional love that I knew I would never be the same. It was a love that was not based on anything I was or could be or that I did or could do. It was just there. Within minutes, I had discovered both death and love.

We took our boat trip. On board, we played chuckaluck. I won a box of chocolates. We sat on deck eating the chocolates, my father's hand on my knee. My sobs were long gone.

When we debarked, we recognized Willie Macher's father, a policeman,

15

among the fishermen on the pier. He had a good catch and gave my father one of his fish to take home with us, wrapped in newspaper.

A dance band was playing polkas as we continued along the pier. We did not forget the cotton candy. I was numbed with sensation and happiness as we made our way to the streetcar. My father sat with the fish in his lap and I stood between his legs, rocking this way and that to the bumpy ride.

We came home triumphantly. The fish was the main object of attention.

"I saw a dead man floating in the water," I announced.

"Is he imagining things again?" my brother asked.

I was not even interested in what my brother might make of our adventures. Instead, I ran into the bedroom and seized my cat Buddha, who was asleep on a pillow. I squeezed her so hard she wriggled from my arms, but I chased her down and hugged her all the more.

The Freedom
to Unfold

By Stuart Brent

THE UNIVERSITY OF CHICAGO PRESS
CHICAGO AND LONDON

MY FATHER'S hands were a miracle of perfection. He could build a house single-handed. He could give you a haircut and butcher a cow. He could fix shoes and make tools and dies. He could farm and irrigate and build the prettiest doll houses in the world. He could make chairs, tables, cabinets; and even as I write this, I am staring at a pipe rack he made for me of hardwood set in a marble base. But it was not his genius as a craftsman that he passed on to me; it was his infatuation with reading.

My father immigrated from Russia in 1901 and through his manual skill became an assistant to the chief tool and die maker at the American Car and Foundry Company in Chicago. Ten years later, he became the chief tool and die maker himself. He was a man of activity, using his physical being all day long. But at night, after supper, he would retire to his favorite chair, open a book, and smoke his pipe. Often in the morning he would arise from bed an hour earlier than necessary to finish reading what he had started the night before, so he could go to work "satisfied." It was a solitary addiction. He could not even discuss his reading with his near neighbors. Cohen, who lived on one side of us, couldn't put two words of English together. Rosenberg, our neighbor on the opposite side, couldn't care less. His only interests were pinochle and drinking tea with lemon.

When I was a child, he often allowed me to go with him in the evening to the new public library that had just been opened on Homan Avenue, a distance of nearly three miles. The streets of Chicago's West Side were poorly-lighted in those days, but it was possible to walk them without fear. My father would check out five books and depart with the books in one hand and my small hand in the other. Usually we walked in total silence until we got to Kobrick's grocery and delicatessen. As we approached the lighted window with its display of candies, bagels, honey cakes, and the salamis hanging from the ceiling, my heart would almost stop. Would father, this night, decide to buy some pipe tobacco then, looking down from his towering height, ask if I would like a sucker or a bag of polly seeds?

In time, we became co-conspirators in the love of reading. Books might not make me a better wage earner, he said, but they could prevent boredom. The experience of reading a good book was like getting unstuck and reaching out toward something entirely new, even though you still wore the same tie and shirt and met the same people.

But the great beauty of the thing, he said, was that when you are reading

21

you are never alone. For my father, to be *aleyn* (the Yiddish for loneliness) was one of the tragic elements in man's experience.

His favorite writer was Tolstoy. "When you read Dostoevsky," he would say "you descend into a coal mine without a ladder for climbing out. When you read Tolstoy, it's like the sun after living in an ice box."

Anatole France's *Penguin Island* and the criticism of Walter Pater were favorites of his. He liked Scott and Dickens. No one understood Dickens until he had read *Our Mutual Friend*, he said. It would be a grave mistake to die without having read that book. You may be sure I read Dickens until I couldn't see straight.

I became a teen-ager imbued with the desire to read everything, to know everything, to be everything. With the advent of the depression, the fulfillment of these modest ambitions required considerable ingenuity. The entire atmosphere of our household was altered. First, my sister, her husband, and two children moved in. Her husband had lost his job after 18 years as a pants cutter at Hart, Schaffner, and Marx. Then, my brother, who was a salesman for the wholesale division of Marshall Field, lost his job, so he, his wife, and three children joined our crowded household. Now the only place to read was either in the bathroom or the public library.

Even during these difficult and sometimes tragic years, there were evenings filled with affection and fun. Everyone crowded into the big kitchen and then, between tea and sweet cakes and perhaps a drop or two or even three of sweet home-made wine, they would talk and tell deprecatory tales of human stupidity, laughing and crying at the same time. The warmth and marvel of those days have never left me.

I was seldom without a book. I read walking along the street; I read standing up, sitting down; I read and read. Before the depression and the great influx of family members, the very best time to read was on Saturday mornings. Normally my mother baked on Friday and she had a genius for failing to remember that something was in the oven. So if I was lucky, there would be plenty of cookies, cake, or strudel left, slightly burned, that nobody else would touch. But I loved it. Then, too, the house was strangely still on Saturday mornings. No one was home and I could turn up the volume on the phonograph as loudly as I wished and sit and listen and read and eat cake. It was wonderful.

When reading became out of the question at home, I simply went to one of the two public libraries within walking distance. I liked best the one known as the Douglas Park branch. It was newer, the seats more comfortable, the selection of books better.

While my remarkable father was responsible for my early love of books, Jesse Feldman, my teacher, in senior high school literature, served to transform that love into an enduring and ever more passionate affair. His enthusiasm supported my own and at the same time held the key to the wealth of possibilities that literature offers.

Through Jesse I learned that difference between a good book and a bad book. A good book is, very simply, a revealing book. A bad book is bad because it is dull. Its author is obviously lying, not necessarily by purveying misinformation, but because he lards his work with any information that falls to hand—a sort of narrative treatment of the encyclopedia. A good book stirs your soul. You find yourself lost, not in a world of fantasy, but in a world where everything is understood.

Nobody can get along without an interior life. The soul must be fed or something ugly and antihuman fills the void. Spiritual nourishment is not a rill, apart from everyday necessity. The everyday and the ultimate expression of man do not exist apart. The Irish poet and playwright J. M. Synge remarked: "When men lose their poetic feeling for ordinary life and cannot write poetry of ordinary things, their exalted poetry is likely to lose its strength of exaltation, in the way men cease to build beautiful churches when they have lost happiness in building shops."

So many years have passed since my father started me in reading as a way of life, marking a passage in a letter from Melville to Hawthorne, his workman's hands caressing the page. "My development," Melville wrote "has been all within a few years past. Until I was 25 I had no development at all. From my 25th year I date my life. Three weeks have scarcely passed, at any time between then and now, that I have not unfolded within myself." How proud I was to have got an earlier start!

I think of those days when my hair was long and I wore the only pair of pants I had until they were in shreds. I used to sit in the classroom with my overcoat on so that the patches on my behind would not show or stay in the library until closing time was called. Then I'd go out into the solitary night, walking thoughtfully home. I didn't want money, success, or recognition. I didn't want a single thing from anybody. I wanted only to be alone, to read, to think, to unfold.

23

Kicking the

SMOKING HABIT

By Stuart Brent

UNIVERSITY OF CHICAGO PRESS

CHICAGO   LONDON

Foreword

THE *following material originally appeared in the form of two articles, the first
of which was published in the January 15, 1964, issue of the* CHICAGO DAILY
NEWS *and the second in the January 17, 1965, issue of the* CHICAGO TRIBUNE.
They are reprinted with the permission of theses two publications.

*For the encouragement of the reader who wishes to kick HIS smoking habit,
the writer can report that as of October, 1969, he remains true to his resolve,
with lungs unsullied except by the polluted air of his Favorite City.*

It had been a good party and when the last guest was gone I sat down amid the usual debris of social eating and drinking and reached for a cigaret—a gesture I had been making from forty to sixty times a day for the past twenty years.

The fact that I stopped in mid-gesture was not due to any gnawing sense of guilt or sudden concern about my health. As a matter of fact, I had recently had a thorough physical examination and been pronounced in the pink of condition. Probably the most immediate factor was the general state of the membranes of my mouth, which at this hour of the early morning suggested that I had been celebrating the new year by chewing old socks.

One more cigaret was not really an inviting prospect at all. It would just be plain foolishness. What better time to conclude a relationship with a totally unnecessary habit, and a damaging one at that?

I went to bed with a feeling of hope and awoke late in the morning with secret determination. As the day progressed, however, I came to the realization that a holiday is not the best time to begin a new way of life. The day could only be described as a long one—it seemed to stretch before me forever.

I began looking frantically for things to do. I straightened drawers, organized old correspondence, cleaned brushes.

None of my family seemed to know that I had stopped smoking, but it was recognized that I was acting strangely.

Little did they know, however, that I was also engaged in outlandish soliloquies: "I am the center of the universe. The sun is coming up behind me. When it shines bright and strong, will it be pouring its life rays out on a maggot or a man?"

I could see myself on trial before the entire family, my wife and my two teen-age sons and the four other children of varying ages: Would father succeed in his great undertaking or be condemned before their eyes as an irremediable second-rate individual? And still the day stretched on.

The next day I awoke with a feeling of being under attack. All the forces of evil had mustered themselves to destroy me. My habit had been established in its most vicious form, with the smoking of a cigaret immediately upon awakening.

Fighting the hideous pattern, I got out of bed with the realization that I was involved in an enormous drama. After breakfast I felt a bit better, although the coffee without a cigaret tasted absolutely terrible. By eight-thirty I was on the road, driving from the suburb to my shop on Michigan Avenue.

My new feeling about time—its unutterable slowness—had become a phenomenon that I was beginning to savour; I sensed that a single day was an eternity of living. How marvelous!

As I drove, I laughed to myself and kept muttering, "Marvelous, marvelous!" My observation seemed to be incredibly acute, as though I were looking at everything with a naked eye: the billboards, the other cars, and drivers, the buildings, and the road extending ahead to infinity.

I chose the slowest lanes on the Outer Drive and continued to enjoy my capacity for observing things, things I had never noticed before, marvelous qualities all about me.

I was just occupying space, looking and moving in it, but not actually participating.

When I came to a stop light, the most remarkable thing happened: the light took minutes, perhaps hours, to change, and I waited without the slightest impatience. I was undergoing a personality change in which I viewed everything without malice or displeasure. Suddenly I became enormously sorry for everyone in the world who was still under the compulsion of a drug habit.

Somewhat to my amazement, I eventually arrived at the shop, and it was still early morning. I entered the shop and was simply charming to everyone. But as time went on—eternal time—there was torment.

Hunger for food arose to appease my other hunger. I sent out for a hamburger. And then when I had eaten the hamburger, I sent out for candy bars. Twenty-five minutes later, I sent for coffee and a hot dog, and twenty-five minutes after that it was for coffee and doughnuts.

But even this wasn't enough. I had to do something physically to mitigate the pain. That gave me the clue. "Well," I said to myself, "if the striped muscles are involved in it, let's go to work."

So I went downstairs to our basement room where the paperback books are displayed and knocked out all the shelves. After looking at the chaos I had created, I then took the station wagon out to load up with lumber. I am not really very handy, but I realized that the only thing that might save me was to start building shelves. I also began to get angry: How dare this small, white cigaret force me to accept its domination? And the anger helped, as it always does in a fight.

On the third day, I discovered an interesting thing that helped to explain the power of my small, white adversary. It occured to me that its power was not only chemical but also spatial. A satisfaction of smoking lies in the visible extension of one's being into space. This is not just a fancy. Space is an extraordinary thing and we are afraid of it. As the smoke of one's cigaret occupies space and defines it, the individual can believe that he belongs somewhere. He can equate this visible relationship with space with whatever is happening in the real world.

No matter what is going on, the puff of smoke seems to say, "I am here." To me, this observation strikes much more deeply at the core of what the cigaret habit contributes to the individual personality, to selfhood, than the supposed satisfaction of an oral stimulus on which the psychiatrists place such high value.

As a matter of fact, doctors and psychiatrists come into my store all of the time (it is located in a medical building). All of them have been aware of the studies relating cigarets to cancer. Nearly all of them have stopped smoking at one time or another, and nearly all of them have come back to it again in one form or another.

I do not really think that the health factors alone would support me in my resolve to quit smoking, although in terms of moral responsibility it is really unreasonable for the father of a family of six (going on seven) to deliberately shorten his probable life span. And if this same father purports to be a man of knowledge and his knowledge teaches him that a practice is definetly injurious, what good is the knowledge if he persists in the practice?

Of course, I could have just switched to a pipe or cigars, with reasonable hope of improving my chances so far as the mortality figures go. But if one is going to break off with a habit, he might as well do it all the way down the middle or not at all. But reasonable or unreasonable, the withdrawal is awful. This is the fact that is really hard to face up to.

It is so easy to look down upon those who have fallen into dope habits that are socially and legally unacceptable and to regard your own socially acceptable (although medically deplored) vice as minor. But when you try to abstain, it is not a minor matter at all. It involves all of your forces. It threatens your total identity.

All at once you are confronted with the meaning of being an addict, and your sympathy reaches out to the whole world of the addicted.

It is not merely a matter of will power or of shaking off the bondage of a certain craving or of surviving the physical pains of withdrawal from a chemical agent. It is a matter of learning to walk again, having abandoned a familiar crutch to identity.

Well, now I am past the fourteenth day, and I have no idea whether I am going to make it.

But I have learned a great deal about myself, and my family, certainly, has discovered all kinds of crazy things about me. In spite of my torments, they are noticing that I laugh more and that I appear less burdened.

They are not fully aware of the struggle I am going through, but they can sense the exhilaration of the self-knowledge that this struggle is yielding for me.

And I must admit that some positive benefits of a physical as well as psychic character are beginning to appear. It has become more of a pleasure to awake in the morning, earlier than usual and with an almost frightening fresh sensation of no longer having an untended birdcage stored in my mouth.

For the first time in sixteen years, I am hungry for breakfast.

There is definitely new hope, and it is this sense of hope that carries me through the day.

For now I am on my own. I must take each day different from the thousands of days that have gone before, when it was impossible for me to do anything of any consequence without a cigaret, lighting another and another, with my identity trailing out through space on a thin line of spreading smoke.

ONE YEAR LATER

Just one year ago, I stopped smoking. The decision seemed only logical. I had been smoking too heavily over the holidays, and the results were unpleasant. Why should I not give up a habit which was unquestionably unhealthy, costly, and unnecessary?

Within a few days, I learned that it was not that simple. I discovered the meaning of addiction, of an attachment that had become part of my whole manner of coping with life. My sense of time and space had become linked with this habit. To see the smoke curling away was to establish my place in space. And my dealings with time were measured as much by the burning of a cigaret as by the clock or the duties of my day.

Without my cigaret, time and space stretched endlessly. But there was an exhilaration in the experience, in having to re-create my relations with world anew. There was an excitement in my daily sense of conquest. Yet, when I wrote about this after the first few weeks of my experience, I had no personal conviction that my will power would sustain me for any considerable length of time. I did not know how it would all turn out.

Today I am happy to report that my resolution of last year is being maintained. I am proud of not having thrown in the sponge. But the difficulties have been far greater than I ever imagined.

To come right down to it, I still miss smoking. But I miss it for reasons I had not known existed. I have mentioned the relation between smoking and time. Smoking filled in the moments of time that were not called for by other actions.

Smoking was time unaccounted for. It turns out that a great deal of life seems to be composed of this kind of time, time that we do not know what to do with. Smoking solves this problem. Stop smoking, and what do you do with time? The answer is known to everyone who has tried to kick the smoking habit: you eat. No other form of gratification is a handier substitute. There is, therefore, on clear consequence of my having been off cigarets for a year: I am eighteen pounds heavier. Since I am not very tall, this is neither becoming nor healthy. I am thus, left with a new problem to deal with and a new vice to kick.

This side effect of giving up smoking tends to obscure what really is involved in the breaking of a habit. In fact, if food becomes a fetish, we only exchange one deep sickness for another. I have come to learn that the problem is not *abstaining* from something or of *replacing* one kind of time killer with another. The challenge is to change one's life *absolutely*.

This realization can come as no small shock. You had thought that you were dealing with a minor vice. In attempting to conquer it, you felt your pride at stake, your self-respect, your esteem in the eyes of your family. But all at once you realize, with something close to terror, that you are not involved merely in a test of will. Why were you trying to kill time? Why were you endeavoring to reduce the space in which you lived to the confines of a trail of smoke? Why were you deadening your perceptions and building the machinery of narcosis into your nervous system? Obviously, you are involved not just with the shaking of a habit, but with the fundamental struggle between light and darkness, life and death.

Only this discovery can make it worthwhile to give up a habit: not because someone tells that the habit may in time kill or injure you, but because you are awakened to a psychic deadening that is already taking place. The habit is but a symptom, and the the only cure is a new interest in life in the most passionate sense.

If we are truly interested in living, we will not be content merely to occupy space or to find ways to kill time while waiting to die. Seeing in yourself the necessity for change, you recognize the profound truth that only changes in man can create changes in society. If you feel challenged to attempt such changes through the tapping of your own resources, your action will arise not out of fear or shame, but out of some interior conviction that it is simply worthwhile.

These are things that are easier to say than to do anything about. I wish that I could report that after having kicked the smoking habit for a year I had become much more tolerant of others, less sensitive to my own failures, greatly improved in disposition, more acute mentally, and less jumpy nervously. This, I fear, is not the case.

Furthermore, the habit has not given me up. A few days ago I had to tell my wife about a dream I had just had. In the dream I was smoking and enjoying it immensely. I was seated near an ash tray filled with half smoked butts. I leaned over the tray and inhaled deeply, with my nostrils almost touching the smoldering butts. My wife did not need to be a psychiatrist to explain the meaning of this wish fullfilment fantasy. Obviously, I am still in battle and the outcome has by no means been determined. If there is one thing I have learned, it is that the gap between theory and practice, between resolutions and behavior, is a hard one. But we cannot deal with facts by ignoring them; in the long run we get exactly what we ask for.

While I miss the pleasures of smoking, I remember what George Eliot wrote: "If you really want to know about your fellow men's miseries, go look at their pleasures." In the struggle with my own misery, I have found at least a glimmer of light that tells me where the battle lies.

One Day at

MASADA

A FRAGMENTATION OF MEMORY

By Stuart Brent

PRIVATELY PRINTED

STUART BRENT BOOKS, INC.

CHICAGO : 1981

The evening of our return from Masada, I sat in the lounge of our hotel in Jerusalem, suffused with the indescribable sense that I would never be lonely again. My soul had a place. My emptiness was filled.

Under any circumstances, this was worth the pilgrimage. But the decision to go was made in a time of trauma. During a six month period, one of my oldest and closest friends had died and I had buried two brothers. When the opportunity to visit Israel arose, I said, "We're going," and immediately wondered why. I had never been much of a Jew, in the religious sense, and my political conscience was non-existent.

As I sat there in the lounge, waiting for our companions to come down for dinner, I still wouldn't have given you two nickels for all the desert in the Middle East. But I knew now that Jerusalem was the Queen of Cities and that God dwelt there. Everything I had read and learned and never felt about my heritage fell into place in a surge of utter peace and tranquility, embracing a feeling for other people one could never articulate, like really falling in love.

The lifelong struggle to prove oneself dropped away in the realization that the dream is now.

My wife, Hope, and I were the only members of our group of travelers who had not visited Israel before. Most had relatives there. None was making the trip for spiritual affirmation. Most of our conversation was about business or shared remembrances of youth on the Chicago West Side.

I had never found commerce and my sense of life as a creative force easy to reconcile, but recalled fondly an old man who did, a fruit peddler from whom I used to buy apples when I opened my first bookstore on Rush Street. (In those days the literary life required something available to munch on at all times, so I kept a large salami sausage and plenty of apples on hand for my clientele). One day I asked him, "Tell me, do you think sex is here to stay?"

"Vi not?" he replied. "It's in a vunderful location!"

Early that March morning, Hope and I, along with two of our friends, had waited outside the hotel for the car that was to take us to Masada. It soon arrived, a Mercedes bus driven by a man named Hyaim who assured us of a pleasant ride and of the benefits of his commentary along the way. A guide's patter was the last thing I wanted, but I held my tongue and determined simply to pay no attention to anything he had to say. This proved not to be difficult, for I already was in a mood of strange detachment, and everything I perceived that clear, cold morning served to further my sense of isolation.

Nor was I really sure why the prospect of seeing the last stronghold against the Romans during a doomed Jewish revolt 2000 years ago had aroused such intense anticipation. According to the legend, the rebels secured themselves at the top of the hill in fortifications so strong that the Romans never penetrated them. At the end of three years of siege, the defenders put themselves to death rather than surrender. The fall of Masada in 73 A.D. marked the end of that era of Jewish independence.

Now we were traveling through the Wilderness of Judah, and whatever the intervening millennia had brought, it was certainly not peace and security. Only days before, while I was in Jerusalem, thirty jews were massacred in the PLO ambush of a bus, provoking an Israeli invasion of Lebanon to clean out the PLO bases. The sense of physical danger was part of the air one breathed in this surreal world of rock and sand and distant summits.

A snatch of insane dialogue from *Alice in Wonderland* flashed through my mind. "I've seen hills compared with which you'd call this a valley," said the Red Queen. "Nonsense," said Alice, "a hill can't be a valley."

We are all stupid fools, I thought, debating what to call what, while the eternal presence all around us goes unseen.

The ancient road to Masada was crowded that day with Israeli soldiers riding in trucks, jeeps, and half-tracks, or on foot with their M16 rifles slung over their shoulders or cradled in their arms. I pictured this same road traveled by caravans of earlier peoples – Phoenicians, Canaanites, Syrians, Babylonians, Hebrews, carrying swords, casting javelins, drawing bows...long ago. All gone, and yet all here, one way and another: the timeless shepherd tending his flock in the green hills (it was spring in Jerusalem), the Arab women, swathed in black dress, engaged in the immemorial act of balancing jugs on their heads while guiding their goats and sheep and children along the side paths of the road. All was bustle, laughter, and yelling and an apparent total indifference to the military presence. That presence, itself, seemed very casual, compared to the discipline of marching ranks which I knew as a soldier in World War II. Regardless of dangers and soldiers, of wars and rumors thereof, everyone on

38

the road seemed bent upon his individual affairs. The noise and the spectacle, in spite of exotic touches, was not unlike that to which I was accustomed as a boy growing up on the West Side of Chicago.

There were frequent check-points and sudden stops, when everyone along the roadway came to a halt, giving me a chance to observe various figures more closely. There were Arabs on camels and donkeys who returned my gaze with fixed stares that were positively hypnotic. One looked at me directly, but it was one distancing gaze, as though from another order of being. A number of priests (I have no idea of what sect), with shaven heads, dressed in long tunics, and carrying long wooden shafts with engraved handles, waved to us and started to shout in some semitic tongue. I was delighted by the strangeness and splendor of it all and began to think like a magician. I started to look for secret signs. Was that old man real whose gaze had passed through me, or was I deceiving myself? My sudden anguish matched the bitter silence of rock and sand.

Abruptly our bus stopped. We were at a check-point and were about to be searched for concealed arms. Peace of mind was not be granted to me, ever. I slumped in my seat like a weary traveller, but was promptly evicted by a group of soldiers bent on examining our vehicle.

While we stood by the bus, a thunderous commotion erupted as a herd of cows was driven across the road, surmounted in their midst by a bull humping a running heifer, his forelegs high on her back, eyes bulging out of his head, all bearing down on us with unslackening speed, cutting finally around us and departing in dust and glory down the side of the roadway.

"There's your sign," said Hope. "It's going to be a good day."

In the distance, Masada loomed like a monster protruding from the sand. It seemed artificial, perhaps a stage prop. Closer at hand, its reality was overwhelming, a 1300 ft outcropping of rock at the eastern edge of the Judean desert overlooking the shore of the Dead Sea. At the base of Masada, our driver let us out and we took the electric lift to the top of the mount. As I looked up, I felt as though everything were dropping away from me: pride, knowledge, even my name. I forgot who I was.

Once at the top, we joined other groups of people and were instructed how to proceed with our tour of the fortress, but my disorientation in time and space continued. The surrounding desert looked pinkish. I picked up some broken shards and let them slip out of my fingers one at a time. They looked pinkish, also. Perhaps it was an effect of the early afternoon sun.

The morning colors on the desert had been yellow and cool blue. In the evening they would be purple. And all day long this landscape of rock and sand was set off by the sky's incredibly brilliant blue. Hope, with one hand in mine and waving the other all about her, said, "Do you mean to tell me that God created all of this out of nothing?"

I had no answer, but was intrigued with the relationship between forbidding landscapes and the spiritual dimension: Moses going off into the wilderness. Jesus and the Buddha. All going off, to return to the human circle with messages gleaned from their withdrawal into loneliness.

We followed the remnants of a colonnade where a synagogue once stood, then entered an area where the baths were located, the elaborate plan of which could be reconstructed in the imagination as one viewed intricate mosaic floors, fragments of walls, and recumbent columns and arches suggesting graceful perspectives. A small sign bore a translation which read: Admittance is open to all. The thought of all this bathing of bodies in the distant past, this ruined monument to the human desire to be clean, struck me as infinitely touching.

I'd better be careful, I thought. Who knows what yesterdays are lurking around these corners. Here was a chamber some of those brave Jews occupied. What did they talk about? Possibly about the ramp, 645 feet long and 400 feet high, the Romans were building. Or about the ultimate destruction which was the only prospect their future offered. Or perhaps about none of these things. Was it time to take a bath?

Around a corner and down some stairs were the remains of a storage place for food and nearby a rock on which I sat to collect my thoughts. Beyond the granary, I saw a man approaching me. He wore a turban, his beard was grey, and he looked very old. He came close to me, bent down, closed his eyes, then opened them with an expression of weariness and sadness beyond description. I sat very still and he said, in perfect English, "There are things that happen beyond the will of man." With that he left. I called to Hope. By the time she reached my side, the old man had disappeared. Together we searched everywhere but couldn't find him. It was very unnerving!

Finally Hope said, "Relax. We have to get back to Jerusalem for supper. Watch yourself and stop having repetitive thoughts."

I felt hurt and wondered what I had been saying.

"I mean," she said, her grey eyes widening, "don't become possessed, or

40

should I say obsessed? We are like tracker come to look at the ancient past. We are the living present and what you see is from the dim past. Leave it at that."

I sat for a while and stared silently at the people passing us by. Still Masada kept its hold on me. On Masada heaven and earth did seem closer. I rose and stood against a pillar and for minutes lifted my head to the sun, letting it beat down on me. I was without conflict, without confusion. I knew I belonged. I remembered Goethe's motto: Become what you are. My individuality, which I always found to be so precious, was melting – was it the sun or the geography? I felt great and small at the same time. Timelessness. All seemed timeless. Yet all about us was the bustling of noisy people, pointing out historic facts to one another and talking in every language conceivable. I saw them moving about us as from a vast distance, like shifting sands and shimmering waves. I knew I once lived here before. In another life, another time, I was one of those Hebrew soldiers who died so long ago.

We went on to examine other rooms, other bath houses, other storage bins. I was being consumed with an enormous enthusiasm, at times completely on fire with a wild joy, as if the whole history of Masada were blazing inside my chest. How should I respond? Should I become a Jeremiah, go back to America and warn everyone that a catastrophe is hanging over our heads?

If so, why was I not being "called?" I was ready, waiting for the sign, the mysterious flash in the sky, the signal from one of the men hurrying past me. Over and again I muttered, "I am ready. I am ready. I will give up everything just for a sign, a telling, a finger, a nod, a wink, any trifle." Nothing.

Since my first day in Jerusalem, I had developed obsessive anxieties and my congenital nervousness had, in fact, accelerated to such an alarming degree that I found it hard to eat; my hands shook so badly that I often could not lift a spoon or a cup to my mouth. I once even dropped a tray of food. It was very embarrassing. Discouraged, I bent down and picked up more of the shards that littered the floor of the fortress. I straightened up slowly, fingering the clay fragments, then allowing them to slip from my fingers and fall again to the ground. As they clattered down, I heard all the voices in the world speaking at once. My hands stopped shaking. I was without conflict or confusion. I knew I belonged. And I knew the world

41

was not a prize for anyone, but a gift for all.

Our friend, Jordan, approached. "I think the bookstore ought to be here, Stuart," he said, pointing to a place about twenty yards from where we stood, "and Ted's lumber yard ought to be over there." Ted was another member of our tour group.

"Why not?" I said. "It's a great location!"

Mr. Toast:

Like All Dogs,
He Was Much More

By Stuart Brent

CHICAGO TRIBUNE
MAGAZINE

THE DOG of the house is gone, dead of cancer at age 13. There will be other dogs in this house-hold, but we will not know them in quite the same way, for we cannot share with them the experiences of the past decade that we shared with Toast. His affectionate responsiveness was a part of our being, and at the same time his individuality extended our capacity for kinship with all living things.

His favorite spot was in front of the fireplace, and in the last few months before he died, he was there more often than not.

He looked well. Oh, his muzzle was turning grey and he was lame in one leg and he had a little trouble getting in and out of the station wagon. Also, he was quite deaf.

But until nearly the end, he was strong and active and practiced the art of the retriever with unfailing perfection. No ball was tossed into the air or stick was thrown down the ravine that was not promptly recovered and returned by Mr. Toast.

David, the oldest of our eight children, used to become greatly annoyed when people spoke of Toast as "almost human." They meant well, But the wonderful thing about Toast was that he was a superb *animal*. He wasn't an imitation, "almost" man. He was a dog and gave what only a dog could offer.

My wife, Hope, and I bought him on a cold January night in 1958. We had a flat tire en route and I lost the way several times. Still, we persisted and ultimately found the home in Northbrook that housed the future protector of the Brent family.

We were ushered down into the basement, part of which was fenced off with wire mesh. The lady of the house opened a kind of make-do door and out came tumbling eight fat golden retriever puppies, bounding and falling over each other. They ran across our feet, rolled behind us, leaped around us, and generally cavorted for perhaps 15 minutes. One puppy kept pawing at my feet until I picked him up, when he promptly kissed me. I passed him to Hope and he kissed her, too. We had been selected.

Settling on an appropriate name was more difficult. We studied the puppy carefully. His coat was reddish brown, his ears were long and curly, his eyes deep brown. He had a short tail and very large paws. Whatever he was named, Mister should be the prefix, we decided, because he was so important looking. And since he was the color of toast, why not call him Mr. Toast?

He was just eight weeks old that winter night when we brought him home. While reading advertisements for dogs, Hope had asked, "Is a golden retriever a little dog?"

"Certainly," I said. "Perfect for an apartment."

Until he was eight months old, his favorite hiding place was beneath our bed. As he became larger, it was an increasing scramble to get under the bed and a virtual impossibility to get out. Finally, he would lift himself up, forcing the mattress to rise, with Hope and me on it!

His increasing stature caused no end of trouble. When he entered the living room, his joyfully wagging tail would sweep the dishes off the coffee table. After suffering innumerable scoldings, he learned to arrest his bounding approach with a frantic skid, at the same time keeping his tail between his legs, a posture both ridiculous and touching.

He continued to grow in strength and beauty and, of course, in size. Ultimately he stood almost 30 inches in height and weighed nearly 90 pounds.

In the summer we would all go up to Bark Point on the Wisconsin Shore of Lake Superior, and there Toast and our children found their true home in the woods and fields and along the lakeshore. Once on our way to the Point we lost Toast, and I later wrote a book about it, "The Strange Disappearance of Mr. Toast" (The Viking Press, 1964). We had all gotten out of the station wagon at a gas station, then piled back in the car without him. We didn't miss him until hours after we reached Bark Point. The odd thing was that most of the children thought they remembered Toast getting out of the car when we arrived at the cottage.

We found him again, of course. Now, in the actual course of events, we have lost him again. The pang of his disappearance is no easier to endure. The illusion of his presence still persists.

Toast in his youth was powerful and active, in his middle years he fathered many magnificent retrievers, and in his declining years he took things easier, slept more, and watched our children grow. He also became something of a literary figure among the younger set, for I wrote two more books about him, mixing real and imaginary adventures. None of the imaginary elements in "Mr. Toast and Wooly Mammoth," and "Mr. Toast and the Secret of Gold Hill" are in any way more wonderful than the realities of Mr. Toast's accomplishments. In fact, some of the things he did, such as swim two miles out into the freezing lake to join me, when I had left him ashore to go fishing, had a note of improbability that made them unsuitable for fiction.

Then there was the day, a few months ago, when Joshua, our 4-year-old, tossed a stick down the ravine for Toast to fetch, and Toast couldn't make it back up the bank. Hope and Amy had to rescue him. Our old dog was dying.

He slept a great deal by the fire. When I bent down and touched him, he-awoke, saw who I was, and nestled his big head in my lap, looking up at me.

"My puppet is sad," Joshua told his nursery school teacher the day after Toast departed.

"Why?" she asked.

"Just sad," he said. "Very sad."

A Love Story

By Stuart Brent

**CHICAGO TRIBUNE
MAGAZINE**

I always let this happen. Two days before Christmas I was crushed by the inevitable and completely unexpected crisis. I had done nothing about my wife's present. It was absurd. I had been in the retail business for 40 years, depending on every holiday season to account for about 70 percent of the year's income.

Without that vital month with its mingling of crass and loving forces impinging on a crazed and helpless populace, I would never have survived in the book business and been able to support a shockingly large family. And here I was in the grip of that recurring nightmare of the demands of love without a gift to give.

It was, of course, 2 o'clock in the morning, the waking hour of unresolved problems. I touched my sleeping wife and thought I felt her body tremble, but perhaps the tremor was my own. I hesitated to waken her, for she had not been well.

Perhaps she was awake. I spoke softly. "What shall I get you for Christmas?"

"Nothing for Christmas," she said.

I turned on the light, and we both sat up.

"But for our anniversary, I'd like my old engagement ring replaced. Only don't spend too much money."

I was stricken again. I had forgotten that on Christmas Day we would have been married 25 years.

The engagement had been short. We were too much in love to protract it. But I knew the ring was important to her and went a little beyond what I could afford to pay: $1,500 for a pear-shaped diamond. But I was so glad I did it, and everything between us went so very well.

We were swept along in time and shared everything together. Nothing was too much of a struggle. Then one day I came home and found her in tears. What could be wrong?

"I lost my ring," she said. She was cleaning it over a lavatory she had forgotten to plug. Of course, the ring slipped. They disassembled the drain, but there was no finding it. I held her and let her cry and promised someday to replace the ring and at the same time wondered how she could have been so careless.

Now it was five children later, two days before Christmas, 2 o'clock in the morning and a moment of both anguish and relief. Restoring the lost ring would be the easiest and gladdest thing I ever did. It would be very simple, I was sure. It would have to be. We both slept well.

The day was soft and bright with light snow, perfect to encourage last-minute shopping. As soon as I reached the book-store, I telephoned my friend, Hugo Spencer, at Tiffany's. "You know how busy I am," I told him. "I can't come in this morning, but I must have a pear-shaped diamond ring. Not too dear, but beautiful and wrapped as a gift." And I described the lost ring as well as I could.

"I'll bring it over myself," Mr. Spencer assured me. Business was as good as I had anticipated, and I had all but forgotten the urgent quest for the ring when I received a phone call from Spencer.

"We are having one sent to us by air today from New York," he said. "You should have it by the end of the day."

"Wonderful. Thank you."

It was near closing time when Spencer hustled into the bookstore looking rather overearnest. He carried a small package and some papers. "Here it is," he said. "And the powers that be have asked if you would please fill out another charge account application. I guess they need more information that we have on file."

"Call the president of my bank," I said, and took the package. I thrust it into a trouser pocket and strolled aggressively through the store without caring whether the resulting effect appeared unseemly.

I carried the gift home, excited and pleased with myself, but keeping it concealed. Long after we were in bed, I felt my wife moving about and whispered, "Would you like to see your anniversary present?"

"Yes, please. Yes!"

I turned on the light, got up and retrieved the box and stood before her in my nightshirt. She propped herself up, and I first handed her the little note I had written, then the box. There was a long silence as she untied the ribbon. I had not looked at the ring and for the first time began to wonder what I had done. "No matter," I assured myself. "There is only one way to deal with difficulties. Disregard them and go ahead."

"It's just right," I said. "Just like the old one."

"Well, we'll see," she said slowly. She arose and, taking my hand, led me down stairs to the library where, amid a pile of ephemeral publications, she uncovered a Tiffany catalog with laminated blue covers containing illustrated data on mineral treasure. Sure enough, there were pages of pear-shaped diamonds of varied qualifications and settings. I felt a paralysis compounded of terror and love.

"My God!" she cried. "Do you know what this ring costs?"

"No, I said, paralysis changing to vertigo. I thought I knew, but now I knew that I didn't.

"Take a look."

"I can't actually see."

She laughed and her gray-blue eyes sparkled with delight. "Sixty-four thousand dollars!"

I had discussed the price with Spencer on the phone. What I heard was "four thousand dollars." What preceded it must have somehow faded over the wire. She who was so precious to me—who daily was more precious—spun before my eyes, the diamond princess. A strange heat suffused me, beginning with the naked feet and spreading upward. "I am ruined," I thought. "But I must work it out somehow."

The illness that had recently plagued her seemed stripped away, and she was glowing. "If I didn't love you, I'd keep it," she said. "You must take it back."

The following morning I walked briskly up the Avenue under a brilliant sky to the golden doorway of Tiffany's. "I was expecting you," said Mr. Spencer, who stood near the entrance. "I'm sorrier about this than I can tell you. I misunderstood you."

"You know, I really thought you did," Spencer said. And the two men, much to their astonishment, hugged on another vigorously.

Stuart Brent
Collecting
Modern
Literature

By Stuart Brent

UNIVERSITY OF CHICAGO PRESS

CHICAGO LONDON

57

IN THE SUMMER OF 1946, I opened the Seven Stairs Book and Record Shop in a converted brownstone residence on Rush Street. Shortly thereafter, I met a true book collector. I wouldn't have guessed it had he not so identified himself upon entering the shop. Although it was a pleasant early fall day, he wore several layers of coats, and beneath these were an indeterminate number of sweaters. His trousers hung at least six inches too short above his workman's shoes, the brim of his black hat rested on his glasses, and he carried a suitcase.

Since I had gone into business with only three hundred dollars worth of books my stock was limited. However, a kindly magazine editor, Ben Kartman, had given me about 500 books to help fill the shelves, and it was to these that my bibliomaniac devoted his attention. He chose two books, paid me, opened his suitcase, shoved the books in with a quick, deft hand, and departed. I watched him take his eccentric course down the street, swaying as he changed the heavy case from hand to hand.

Much later, after I had grown to know him, I encountered him near the Newberry Library. He told me he lived close at hand. Would I like to see some of his treasures? I hesitated, but of course I was curious. I followed him to the fifth floor of an old townhouse. He opened the door upon an overwhelming scene: books and bundles of books from floor to ceiling. Another door opened into a small bedroom; and this room was also filled with books, on the bed, under the bed, up the walls, covering the windows, books everywhere. It seemed as though all the books in the world (someone once told me there are 50 million titles) had been compressed into this miserable apartment. The effect was terribly oppressive, but the collection was not trash.

"Martin," I said, "who, looking at you, would think you were so rich...so rich and so crazy?"

"Listen," he said, "the life of the spirit is not a commercial transaction."

Which is true. Although, when this man, to whom human society was of virtually no concern, died about ten years ago, his library was disposed of for better than $700,000.

The acquisitive spirit of the collector may have its negative, even pathological, aspects. But, impure or not, book collecting at its best is an affair of the heart. You collect books because you love them, both as tactile objects and as expressions of human spirit.

There is nothing, absolutely nothing, like the experience of opening or touching a book: its always unexpected reality, the surprise of its individuality, its relationship to the mind and spirit of someone who was great or who is shaping our thought and perception today.

Well-chosen books can also be an investment that grows in value as the years go by, and their scarcity in the market place increases. But before you decide to collect first editions as a hedge against inflation, remember Wordsworth's admonition: "Bring with you a heart that watches and receives." Collect only what you love.

Those who have the funds and inclination to seek out and purchase incunabula (or the first editions of notable writers in centuries prior to our own) need no advice from me. Even Harry Levin's definition of Modernism as an epoch bounded by T. S. Eliot at one end and Beckett at the other will (if you adopt this as your province) send you to the rare-book shops and auction houses. A first edition of Eliot's *The Wasteland* with the original salmon-colored dust jacket is now worth between $600 and $800, according to the latest edition of Van Allen Bradley's indispensable *The Book Collector's Handbook of Values* (Putnam). And Beckett's *Waiting for Godot* will cost you from $50 to $75 for the 1954 New York edition.

To collect authors who have already assumed their places in literary history is a fine thing. But even better, and surely much easier on the pocketbook, is to make your own choice of current writers and start collecting them. I am not a rarebook dealer, but over the past 25 years my customers have purchased hundreds of books, at retail price, which have since multiplied greatly in value.

The first time Malcolm Cowley came into my shop, he was amazed to find that I had three copies on the shelf of his book of poems, *Blue Juniata*. That led to a wonderful conversation that later turned up in his book, *The Literary Situation in the United States*. Today the volume of poems is worth between $75 and $100!

In the early days of my shop off Rush Street, we held frequent autographing cocktail parties for Nelson Algren, selling copies of *The Neon Wilderness* in the hope of encouraging his publisher to increase the advances on Nelson's work in progress, *The Man with the Golden Arm*. Today those first-edition copies of *The Neon Wilderness* (1947), in dust jacket, command from $35 to $50. So does *The Man with the Golden Arm*. And a first edition of Nelson's first Book, *Somebody in Boots* (1935), is worth $200.

Maybe you are a collector without knowing it. If you have been a constant reader and buyer of books over the years, go to your bookshelves and see if you have first printings of works by any of the following authors: Saul Bellow, Graham Greene, Truman Capote, Tennessee Williams, Ernest Hemingway, John Steinbeck, Norman Mailer, Thomas Wolfe, F. Scott Fitzgerald, Theodore Dreiser, Robert Frost, Edmund Wilson, John Barth. This is an arbitrary list and here is an equally arbitrary sampling of values first editions of the works of such authors already command:

John Steinbeck, *Tortilla Flat* (1935), first edition in dust jacket, $100 to $135.

Graham Greene, *Brighton Rock* (1938), red cloth, first edition, $100 to $150.

Saul Bellow, *Dangling Man* (1944), first edition, $150 to $175.

Truman Capote, *Other Voices, Other Rooms* (1948), first edition, $50 to $75.

Tennessee Williams, *One Arm and Other Stories* (1948), boxed, one of 50 signed, $300 to $500.

Norman Mailer, *The Naked and the Dead* (1948), advance copy in printed wrapper, $150.

Another area of collecting, with surprising investment opportunities, is provided by art books. *The Lithographs*, Volume I, of Marc Chagall, published by George Braziller, which I sold fifteen years ago for $25, is now worth $1,500. The second volume of the series is valued at $1,000. The first edition of the Andrew Wyeth, published seven years ago by Houghton Mifflin for $75, received a bid of $1,000 last year at a Boston auction.

Now let me make a suggestion. If you feel the urge to build a collection of modern books, forget about the market quotation. Collect the works only of those writers and creative artists for whom you feel an affinity. Make a serious effort to obtain signed copies of first editions, if at all possible (and it usually is—your bookdealer can help you in this). Over a period of time, your efforts will almost certainly yield three benefits:

1. By collecting that which you love, you will strengthen and enrich the most important thing you have, your personal identity. Therein lies the intense, Biblical meaning of your own name.

2. If your taste and imagination are at all profound, the personal library you thus develop is likely to appreciate considerably in market value and to become a worthwhile legacy.

*   3.   By joining the ranks of those who demand from the publishing industry a product of enduring value, you will be contributing to the maintenance of standards in book production at a critical time in the history of print. The sewn, hard-cover book, excellent in typography and design, will simply cease to exist without a buying public.*

So, by all means, open yourself to the experience of collecting books, not as commodities, but as spiritual artifacts, closely related to your very being and to the worth and dignity of mankind.

The Stuart Brent
List of Books

By Stuart Brent

PUBLISHED BY
SIMON & SCHUSTER

It occurs to me with a shock that for forty years I have been a bookseller – forty years of seeking and selling good books! My idea of hell is, quite simply, a life without books. And heaven? Peeling back the years, I see myself on a Saturday morning in my mother's big kitchen, sitting at the table reading Thomas Hardy's *Tess of the D'Urbervilles*. Beside me was a bowl of mandelbrot. So I ate and read. That was heaven!

My father used to say: "The best smell is that of bread, the best savour that of salt, the best love that of children, the best of life – a book." I was 19 when I started reading Hardy, the real beginning of my life in books. My book *The Seven Stairs* (available in paperback) tells about this and my early adventures as a bookseller.

List of 100 this or that exert curious fascination. Recently I have been running up my personal lists of 100 "best books" – not necessarily the books that critics say are masterpieces or teachers require you to read or *The New York Times* recommends, but books that have had special meaning for me. The importance of a book lies in the process it initiates in the reader. As Proust said: "Reading is at the threshold of spiritual life; it can introduce us to it; it does not constitute it."

Often the circumstances under which we read have an important part in the process. With this in mind, I have not only chosen my 100 best books, but also suggested the places or conditions that may be most favorable for reading them. Otherwise I shall make no comment on my selections; if you enjoy them, you will have your own reasons.

In any case, here we go with Brent's 100 favorites.

Reading While Eating Alone

By

_____ 1. Him with His Foot in His Mouth   *Saul Bellow*
(cloth 15.95)

_____ 2. Portrait of Jennie   *Robert Nathan*
(cloth 11.95)

_____ 3. A Handful of Dust   *Evelyn Waugh*
(cloth 10.95   paper 6.95)

_____ 4. Remembrance of Things Past,
Vol. 1   *Marcel Proust*
(cloth 25.00   paper 13.95)

_____ 5. The Informal Heart   *Bruno Bettelheim*
(cloth 17.95   paper 4.50)

_____ 6. The Seven Pillars of Wisdom   *T.E. Lawrence*
(paper 7.95)

_____ 7. The Red and the Black   *Stendahl.*
(paper 3.95)

_____ 8. Alain on Happiness   *Alain*
(cloth 10.50   paper 4.95)

_____ 9. Magic Mountain   *Thomas Mann*
(cloth 20.50   paper 6.95)

_____ 10. Caine Mutiny   *Herman Wouk*
(cloth 15.95   paper 4.95)

Reading While Taking a Bath

By

____ 1. Our Mutual Friend   *Charles Dickens*
          (paper 4.95)

____ 2. Memoirs of Hadrian   *Marguerite Yourcenar*
          (cloth 17.95   paper 10.95)

____ 3. Madame Bovary   *Gustave Flaubert*
          (cloth 6.95   paper 2.95)

____ 4. Nana   *Emile Zola*
          (paper 4.95)

____ 5. Turn the Screw   *Henry James*
          (paper 1.95)

____ 6. Dubliners   *James Joyce*
          (cloth 17.50   paper 5.95)

____ 7. Green Mansions   *W.H. Hudson*
          (paper 1.50)

____ 8. Collected Stories of
          John O'Hara   *John O'Hara*
          (cloth 19.95)

____ 9. The Stories of John Cheever   *John Cheever*
          (cloth 20.00   paper 3.95)

____ 10. Miss Lonelyhearts   *Nathaniel West*
          (paper 4.95)

Reading in Bed   By

____ 1. Obscure Desinies   *Willa Cather*
        (paper 4.95)

____ 2. The Slave   *Isaac Bashevis Singer*
        (paper 4.95)

____ 3. Arrow in the Blue   *Arthur Koestler*
        (cloth 14.95)

____ 4. Someone Like You   *Roald Dahl*
        (cloth 10.00)

____ 5. The Fifth Business   *Robertson Davies*
        (paper 4.95)

____ 6. Herzog   *Saul Bellow*
        (cloth 12.95   paper 4.95)

____ 7. The Lonely Passion of
        Judith Hearne   *Brian Moore*
        (paper 6.95)

____ 8. The Cannibal Galaxy   *Cynthia Ozick*
        (cloth 11.95   paper 7.95)

____ 9. King Solomon's Mines   *H Rider Haggard*
        (paper 2.25)

____ 10. In Bluebeard's Castle   *George Steiner*
         (paper 6.95)

70

Reading in the Country

By

____ 1. The Bridges of San Luis Rey
(cloth 12.95   paper 3.50)

Thronton Wilder

____ 2. Barchester Towers
(cloth 9.95   paper 4.95)

Anthony Trollope

____ 3. Anna Karenina
(cloth 9.95   paper 4.95)

Leo Tolstoy

____ 4. Mrs. Dalloway
(cloth 11.95   paper 3.95)

Virginia Woolf

____ 5. The Trial
(cloth 13.50   paper 5.45)

Franz Kafka

____ 6. Tender is the Night
(cloth 17.50   paper 5.95)

F. Scott Fitzgerald

____ 7. Sister Carrie
(paper 3.95)

Theodore Dreiser

____ 8. Candide
(paper 1.95)

Voltaire

____ 9. Grapes of Wrath
(cloth 20.00   paper 3.95)

John Steinbeck

____ 10. For Whom the Bell Tolls
(cloth 14.95   paper 4.95)

Ernest Hemingway

Reading in a Plane or Train   By

___ 1. Will's Boy   *Wright Morris*
        (cloth 12.95   paper 5.95)

___ 2. The Moon and Sixpence   *W. Somerset Maugham*
        (paper 3.95)

___ 3. Gift from the Seas   *Anne Morrow Lindbergh*
        (cloth 7.95   paper 2.95)

___ 4. Siddhartha   *Hermann Hesse*
        (cloth 16.96   paper 2.95)

___ 5. Ficciones   *Jorge Luis Borges*
        (paper 6.95)

___ 6. Stories   *Katherine Mansfield*
        (cloth 20.00   paper 4.95)

___ 7. The Screwtape Letters   *C.S. Lewis*
        (cloth 9.95   paper 2.95)

___ 8. The Art of Loving   *Erich Fromm*
        (cloth 11.95   paper 3.95)

___ 9. The Complete Sherlock Holmes   *Arthur Conan Doyle*
        (cloth 15.95)

___ 10. The Secret Agent   *Joseph Conrad*
        (paper 4.95)

Reading in a Garden By

____ 1. The Little Prince *Antoine de Saint-Exupery*
    (cloth 7.95   paper 1.95)

____ 2. Hamlet: *William Shakespeare*
    Frailty, Thy Name Is Woman, Act I,Scene ii,
    To Be or Not to Be, Act III,Scene i
    (cloth 19.95   paper 2.25)

____ 3. King Lear: *Willima Shakespeare*
    Lear and Cordelia, Act I, Scene vii
    (cloth 19.95 paper 2.25)

____ 4. Crabbed Age and Youth from
    The Passionate Pilgrim *William Shakespeare*
    (cloth 19.95   paper 2.95)

____ 5. Past Reason Hunted from
    The Sonnets, CXXIX *William Shakespeare*
    (cloth 19.95   paper 2.95)

____ 6. Love's Philosophy from
    Collected Poems of Shelley *Percy B. Shelley*
    (cloth 30.00   paper 5.95)

____ 7. Faust and Margaret from Faust,
    Part One *J.W. von Goethe*
    (paper 3.50)

____ 8. A Parable from Collected Stories *Oscar Wilde*
    (cloth 19.95   paper 3.95)

____ 9. Martin Eden *Jack London*
    (paper 4.95)

____ 10. Essays *Ralph Waldo Emerson*
    (cloth 9.95 paper 3.95)

Reading by the Lake

_____ 1. The Stranger   *Albert Camus*
(cloth 10.95   paper 2.95)

_____ 2. A High Wind in Jamaica   *Richard Hughes*
(paper 2.95)

_____ 3. Pericles' Funeral Oration   *Thucydides*
(paper 3.25)

_____ 4. The Colossus of Maroussi   *Henry Miller*
(paper 5.25)

_____ 5. A Separate Peace   *John Knowles*
(cloth 13.95   paper 2.95)

_____ 6. The Long Goodbye   *Raymond Chandler*
(paper 2.25)

_____ 7. The Liberal Imagination   *Lionel Trilling*
(cloth 10.00)

_____ 8. The Basic Fault   *Michael Balint*
(cloth 21.50)

_____ 9. The Wound and the Bow   *Edmund Wilson*
(paper 4.95)

_____ 10. Rubaiyat of Omar Khyyam

                                        Translated by *Edward Fitzgerald*
(cloth 8.95   paper 2.95)

Reading When Bored

_____ 1. Modern Man in Search of a Soul   *C.G. Jung*
(paper 2.95)

_____ 2. Humboldt's Gift   *Saul Bellow*
(cloth 12.95   paper 5.95)

_____ 3. The Nine Tailors   *Dorothy Sayers*
(cloth 11.95   paper 3.95)

_____ 4. The Daughter of Time   *Josephine Tey*
(paper 3.95)

_____ 5. The Maltese Falcon   *Dashiell Hammett*
(paper 2.95)

_____ 6. Travels in Arabia Deserta   *Charles M. Doughty*
(paper, 2 volumes, 10.95 each)

_____ 7. Dr. Jekyll and Mr. Hyde   *Robert Louis Stevenson*
(paper 2.95)

_____ 8. The Woman in White   *Wilkie Collins*
(paper 3.95)

_____ 9. Robinson Crusoe   *Daniel Defoe*
(cloth 17.95   paper 2.25)

_____ 10. Captain Horatio Hornblower   *C.S. Forester*
(cloth 12.95)

Reading in Search of Ideas

			By
___	1.	Island (paper 3.50)	*Aldous Huxley*
___	2.	Job (cloth 24.95 paper 7.50)	*Old Testament*
___	3.	Genesis (cloth 24.95 paper 7.50)	*Old Testament*
___	4.	Corinthians (cloth 24.95 paper 7.50)	*New Testament*
___	5.	Irrational Man (paper 5.50)	*William Barrett*
___	6.	Beyond Good and Evil (paper 2.95)	*Friedrich Nietzsche*
___	7.	Man's Search for Himself (cloth 14.95 paper 6.95)	*Rollo May*
___	8.	Ideology and Utopia (paper 4.95)	*Karl Mannheim*
___	9.	The Hero with a Thousand Faces (cloth 33.00 paper 7.95)	*Joseph Campbell*
___	10.	The Varieties of Religious Experience (cloth 6.95 paper 4.95)	*William James*

Reading Just a Good Book

By

_____ 1. Middlemarch
     (cloth 15.95   paper 4.95)
George Eliot

_____ 2. Tom Jones
     (cloth 17.50   paper 3.95)
Henry Fielding

_____ 3. Man's Fate
     (paper 4.95)
Andre Malraux

_____ 4. Maldorer
     (paper 4.95)
Comte de Lautreamont

_____ 5. Bourgeois Anonymous
     (paper 7.95)
Morris Philipson

_____ 6. Civilization and Its Discontents
     (cloth 10.95   paper 2.95)
Sigmund Freud

_____ 7. The Confidential Clerk
     (cloth 9.95   paper 6.95)
T.S. Eliot

_____ 8. Quinlan's Key
     (paper 10.95)
Sterling Quinlan

_____ 9. Adventures of Huckleberry Finn
     (cloth 15.00   paper 1.75)
Mark Twain

_____ 10. Lolita
     (paper 5.95)
Vladimir Nabokov